THE QUEST FOR
EXCALIBUR

BY

ANGELA F. C. LOCASCIO

DORRANCE PUBLISHING CO., INC.
PITTSBURGH, PENNSYLVANIA 15222

All Rights Reserved
Copyright © 2001 by Angela F. C. Locascio
No part of this book may be reproduced or transmitted
in any form or by any means, electronic or mechanical,
including photocopying, recording, or by any information
storage and retrieval system without permission in
writing from the publisher.

ISBN # 0-8059-5016-8
Printed in the United States of America

First Printing

For information or to order additional books, please write:
Dorrance Publishing Co., Inc.
643 Smithfield Street
Pittsburgh, Pennsylvania 15222
U.S.A.
1-800-788-7654

Or visit our website and online catalogue at *www.dorrancepublishing.com*

DEDICATED TO: My loving husband John and my children Andrea and John and my father Anthony Marchese. I give you this story with all my love.

PROLOGUE

EXCALIBUR -SWORD OF FAITH

Excalibur was conceived and created by The Lady of the Lake. She was given into Merlin's trusting hands, with one condition. Only a man with a pure heart and soul could possess Excalibur's protective powers. If she is misused, Excalibur and her powers will be removed from that person. The Lady told Merlin, "Be careful to whom you give the sword, Excalibur. She is a sword of faith and only the faithful can use her. Otherwise, suffer the consequences yourself."

MERLIN-CELTIC LEGENDARY SORCERER

Merlin is the son of Queen Mab, Evil Sorceress. Queen of Black Magic. Raised by a forest woman after the death of his mortal mother. The woman to whom Merlin so tenderly called Auntie Aye raised him until he was eighteen. She raised Merlin to believe in the good of people.

At eighteen years of age Merlin's magic powers developed. Queen Mab came to claim her son. Mab wished his powers to be as black as hers were. Merlin fought back after finding out that Mab killed his biological mother and that his mortal life was conceived by black magic. Merlin learned how to fight his evil mother and therefore she banished him from her forest.

Merlin's powers became great. He became King Uther's guide. Merlin gave Excalibur to Uther. Uther misused Excalibur. Therefore, Merlin locked Excalibur in a stone. Arthur, Uther's son, later proved to be the rightful owner when he pulled the precious sword from the stone. Arthur and Merlin were close from Arthur's birth. Arthur's mother, The Lady Igraine, died soon after Arthur's birth. His father, King Uther, died in battle.

Merlin adopted Arthur. He became his guide in life. Upon Arthur's death Merlin returned EXCALIBUR to The Lady of the Lake.

EXCALIBUR WAS NEVER SEEN AGAIN.

KING ARTHUR PENDRAGON

KING ARTHUR PENDRAGON, legendary British Monarch of Medieval Britain owned Excalibur until his death. He fought the Romans for the HOLY GRAIL, THE CUP USED BY JESUS CHRIST AT THE LAST SUPPER. His attempts failed.

GALAHAD

GALAHAD, son of Sir Lancelot and Lady Elaine of Astolate, was known as the most pure of all King Arthur's Knights. He has been known as the last blood descendant of Joseph of Aramethia. He was the one chosen to find the Holy Grail.

SIR MODRED PENDRAGON

SIR MODRED PENDRAGON, King Arthur Pendragon's illegitimate son. His mother the Lady Morgana, otherwise known as Morgan La Fey, was King Arthur's half sister by their mother The Lady Igraine. Arthur's father seduced and raped Igraine- thereby Arthur's birth came forth. The Lady Morgana wanted the throne, so she seduced her half brother. Since Arthur did not know that this was his sister he allowed the affair to happen.

Modred was conceived from this affair and kept secret from Arthur. One major problem when you mix the same blood and mix it with treachery from a jealous mother is that it is not only genetic suicide but also produces a child with insanity, schizophrenia and all the other casualties he shall inherit growing up.

Unfortunately Modred did not grow up today-maybe his father could have found help for his son and they could have found common ground to live on.

TOURETTE SYNDROME PLUS

Tourette Syndrome Plus as it is known today is also a genetic problem. The gene has not been found which causes this affliction.

Tourette Syndrome causes involuntary movements of the body. The involuntary repetitive movements are called Tics which can make a person, male or female suffering with it, not only uncomfortable with themselves as individuals, but people unfamiliar with their problem could look at them as rude and undisciplined human beings, sometimes even freaks of nature. This disorder can also cause stuttering of words, also known as the cursing brain. (My son does not suffer with this part of it).

Children with Tourette Syndrome have also been diagnosed with ADHD (Attention Deficit Hyperactivity Disorder) and ODD (Oppositional Defiance Disorder) which can cause rage attacks making the person difficult to live with.

FOREWORD

Since I was a girl in High School I have always loved History. The History of King Arthur has always had a special place in my heart. Merlin the Sorcerer has always intrigued me. Sam Neill, the movie actor, starred in the television version "MERLIN". The story inspired me to write this story. It made me remember how much I admired these two men of history. Come with me on "THE QUEST FOR EXCALIBUR". Watch King Arthur and Merlin journey to Camelot. I hope you will fall in love too.

Chapter One

THE ROAD TO CHAOS

The sirens were blaring. Arianna Lawrence lay unconscious in the ambulance. Her husband, Jack Lawrence, sat paralyzed watching the paramedics work on her.

Just one week ago Arianna complained that between his long hours and their sons' behavioral problems at school, Joseph's tutorial schedule and meetings with his social worker, Arianna was completely exhausted. She had no time to breathe and it was showing for a long time. It was Jack's rude awakening as to how much was too much for a single person to handle.

Arianna lay there lifeless, only time and God was to be on her side now.

As the ambulance reached Park General Hospital, Arianna started showing some form of consciousness. Before Jack could think Arianna was wheeled into the emergency room. Her temperature was 94° Fahrenheit and her blood pressure was 180 over 115. She was pale and her skin was clammy to the touch. Her heart was pounding.

Jack watched in horror through the window in the emergency room. Arianna was never sick-it was always either he or the children. Arianna was his rock, his anchor in life. Jack's thoughts were frightening: "What if Arianna dies? How will I raise my children alone? Please God help."

Two hours later Dr. Smith drew out of the room. His face appeared positive. Jack rose from his chair, fear written on his face, his blue eyes dazed. Dr. Smith laid his hand on Jack's quivering shoulder.

"Arianna will be O.K. She's highly exhausted and needs plenty of rest."

Jack felt as though his legs would crumble.

"What the hell happened?" he said, while nervously scratching his head.

"Jack, Arianna suffered from a mini stroke. She is going to be here awhile. She needs plenty of rest."

"You are kidding."

Dr. Smith looked at Jack in anger. "Are you blind? Arianna has been tired for a long time, but you and her family just cannot see it. According to all of you Arianna's not a person but a piece of machinery. Well the machine broke down Jack. Now it's time for all of you to take care of her."

"Doctor Smith can I please see her?"

Jack could not believe what he saw. Arianna was hooked up to an I.V. and a blood pressure monitor. Her once strong face was now ashen. As he kissed her cheek Arianna opened her tearful brown eyes.

The bright lights of this aesthetic room intimidated Arianna. They were too much of a reminder of her mother's death.

"Jack, how did I get here? Are the kids all right?"

Jack stroked Arianna's brown hair.

" The kids are fine, they are with Brenda. You came here in an ambulance. You had a bad headache and passed out. Joseph called me up from the basement and I called 911. I am so sorry, I am so very sorry for not seeing this. All I want you to do is get better."

As Arianna looked at Jack's frightened face all she could think of was the past ten years. In and out of emergency rooms with Jack being sick.

The nurse came to take some blood. The needle hurt. Tests more tests, always afraid of getting sick herself. Funny as she felt the sheets under her weak body she thought "Now the tides are turned."

Doctor Avery Smith stood beside Arianna. Arianna looked into his caring hazel eyes.

"What happened to me?"

"Arianna, fatigue and exhaustion took their toll."

" Please Doc, was it a heart attack?"

"No dear, you had a mini stroke."

Arianna put her face to her hand. It was the one with the intravenous in it. She looked at her hand with tears in her eyes and softly said, "My God, Help."

Dr. Smith held the other hand, and in a reassuring voice said, "He will and so will we."

"Thanks Doc."

Chapter Two

THE ROAD HOME

As the days went by Arianna felt stronger. Her only complaint was a nagging lightheadedness, of which Dr. Smith told her would diminish with renewed strength.

Today was especially great because Arianna's children, Alexis and Joseph, came to visit with her. The children made cards for mom and came with lots of hugs and kisses. Joseph told mommy all about karate and how his new forms were coming. Alexis told mom about the school dance and mostly that she needed mom home. Arianna said, "I'll be home as soon as Dr. Smith says I can."

"Mommy, can you come home today, can you, can you?" Joseph said, with big smiles on his face.

"Not today Joseph."

"Oh Mom!"

When Jack entered the room he had just seen Dr. Smith. With relief written on his face he said, "Arianna, Dr. Smith told me if all goes well you could very well be home by Sunday."

Arianna smiled. For Jack, it had been two long weeks. He finally realized that his wife's job was not an easy one. Maybe he needed to walk in her shoes.

Sunday came and before Jack entered Arianna's room, Dr. Smith grabbed him in the hall for a conference about Arianna's health.

"Jack, listen to me. Arianna has been through a hard time."

"I know Dr. Smith." Jack started rubbing the back of his tense neck.

"Please sit down, there is something you need to know."

"What is it? Is Arianna all right?"

Dr. Smith folded his arms. "Yes, she is fine, but I want to keep her that way."

Dr. Smith sat next to Jack. "Arianna needs a long vacation."

Jack nervously cracked his knuckles.

"I am warning you that if Arianna goes back to her old routine, I'm afraid she just might be back here again."

Jack confessed. "I wish we could Doc, but there aren't any funds to allow such a vacation."

Dr. Smith stood, his caring hazel eyes now looked very annoyed.

"I have one thing to say to you, borrow it, beg for it. If Arianna is more important than money, you will find a way."

Finding a way was always hard for Jack.

Jack entered Arianna's room. Arianna was already dressed and anxious to go home.

"Hey look at you, I can't wait to get you home."

Arianna stood by the sink brushing her long brown hair. "Where are the kids?"

"They're home with Brenda."

"Looks like I've done a good job."
"Arianna, please sit down."
"Oh Doc, what now?"
There were those caring hazel eyes again.
"When you get home, please take it easy."
Arianna stood up.
"OK Doc. NOW PLEASE LET ME GET OUT OF HERE!"
"On one condition, I want you to call my office and make an appointment for a week from now."
"I will, I promise. Let me out of here."

Arianna's homecoming was a happy but exhausting one. Home felt so strange that she felt haunted by memories of two weeks ago when she felt her legs give way from under her, and then waking up in an ambulance. She shivered with fear.

The children were so glad, they made a "Welcome Home" sign, and Alexis baked cupcakes with Brenda for after dinner. Seeing her children's happy faces helped ease the fear.

It was nine o'clock PM. Arianna decided she was going to bed. As she lay there comfortable in her own bed, she looked at her wedding picture and the children's baby pictures, the layout of the room. All her fears rushed to her peaceful soul as though a monster came out of the woodwork and attacked her. She cried herself to sleep.

Jack watched Arianna sleep. His thoughts were on what Dr. Smith said earlier. Did his wife really need a vacation? He had so much work at his job, how could he leave? Jack is the type of man married to two people-one his job, two his wife. Which one does he hold closer to his heart?

Arianna was constantly asking to go away, but the answers were only no. It was always the same: Jack's illness, the job, the kids, etc. etc.

Jack has an immune disorder, which requires a special type of care. Can he find a hospital away from home, which can help him? Jack is the type of man who lives in denial. He has trouble dealing with reality and his own demons.

Jack has "A Common Variable Immune Deficiency." He needs a blood product called Sandoglobulin in order to sustain his "T" CELLS to fight infection, fatal or otherwise. It has to be infused every three weeks.

This simply means a nurse comes to their house and for three to four hours Jack gets hooked up. So in order for Jack to go away he would have to have his Doctor contact a hospital abroad and get the medical attention he so desperately needs. Jack never really liked that idea at all and Arianna of course always has her dreams put on hold.

Arianna loves to read. Since she was a girl she would read books about sunken ships to books about Kings, Queens and Knights fighting Warlords and Dragons. There were times when she would finish a book and wonder what it would be like to go where her stories took her. If only in her imagination, could she sit in a forest in England and imagine a Knight slaying a Dragon for her honor? Or, maybe a passenger on a sinking ship? Her uncles were on the Titanic. How horrible that night was for them. They were not found. Would she survive? Could she be brave?

Reality always took its toll. LIFE must be dealt with. So the books and the dreams were put on the shelf again. Arianna constantly felt she was competing with Jack's job, his illness and her son Joseph's Tourette's Syndrome, combined with ADHD (Attention Deficit Hyperactivity Disorder/Defiance Disorder)-another reality. Meetings with social workers every two weeks, and lets not forget the psychiatrist once a week, and his daily medication. Joseph also attended behavior modification classes. When is there an end?

There are things in the house she would like to do. Maybe renovate the kitchen, paint the living room, and even maybe purchase some new chairs. But alas, school tuition, dance and karate lessons all took precedence.

At times, Arianna would think about her high school days. What ever happened to the writer in her? Arianna was going to write great books and turn them all into screenplays. Maybe even act in her own stories. It is as though they all left her in a cloud of dust. As though her endless struggles had been their crematory.

The kids knew mom was feeling low. Alexis made Mom beautiful cards that simply read "I LOVE YOU MOM". A big kiss went with that. Joseph drew a happy face on a piece of computer paper. It read "MOMMY, I MISSED YOU A BUNCH". Arianna cried and said she missed them too.

A week had passed so quickly. Jack went back to work. He had taken a couple of days off. Getting back in the routine was hard. Arianna felt as though her job she had done so well for so long was now the hardest thing. She now realized how sick she had gotten. In her heart she knew she was strong willed and getting back into the quick of things would happen one day at a time.

Monday had finally arrived. Arianna had a three o'clock appointment with Dr. Smith. She picked the kids up at school and went to the office. The minute she opened the doors her anxiety levels swelled. Her heart would not stop racing. She tried to read a magazine article but she found herself wondering what Dr. Smith was going to say about her. Fear took control again. The kids acting like kids were antsy waiting for mom, and Arianna started to feel strange again.

Dr. Smith called her in, took one look at her, took his glasses off those caring eyes and yelled, "I knew that if I sent you home you would not rest!"

Arianna laughed. "On what planet do I find rest? I have no one to depend upon. I'm lucky Brenda takes the kids Thursday and Friday when I work."

Dr. Smith stood there making notes on Arianna's chart and looked up from his glasses. "I didn't know you worked. What do you do?"

"I'm a hairdresser, and a good one too."

"You sound proud of your work."

Dr. Smith placed the blood pressure armband on Arianna's left arm.

"Actually, I've been thinking of taking over the shop. My boss is retiring------ Do you have to make that thing so tight?"

"Never mind young lady."

"Oh excuse me. I'm the one in pain and you say never mind." Arianna watched the numbers go up then down.

"Now tell me it doesn't hurt that much."

"No, not really. So what's the verdict?"

Dr. Smith took a deep breath. "Your pressure is 140 over 90. It's good, but I'd like to see it at least ten points lower. I would like to see you take it easy."

5

"Sure, that's easy for you to say."

Dr. Smith looked at Arianna's aggravated expression, realizing he had struck a nerve. He realized he never knew that much about this woman. In the ten years the Lawrence family had been his patients he knew everything about Jack, Alexis and Joseph, but somehow Arianna remained a mystery. Arianna always seemed so strong.

"Arianna, please sit down."

"Is everything OK?"

"Yes, everything is just fine."

Dr. Smith put his glasses in his pocket. "I have one question."

Arianna looked puzzled.

"Why did you neglect to come in sooner? You take care of your family so carefully…"

"Please Doc the kids are waiting."

"You know what I am about to say. Why did you hide this from me?"

Arianna grew angry. She got up to leave, Dr. Smith grabbed her arm---"I want an answer!"

She looked at Dr. Smith's hand on her arm. "Dr. Smith let go."

"HIDE, IS THAT WHAT YOU THINK? Do you know what it is like to have a son like Joseph? There are days when he has me to the point of no return. His behavioral problems and Tourette's cause problems with family and sitters. We can't go to too many places-people look at Joseph as though he is some freak show."

Dr. Smith looked at Arianna and finally started to understand. "The people I try and get some help from are not dependable or responsible enough."

"What about family?"

"You must be joking-they all make excuses. They all think this is in Jack's and my imagination. Why? Oh it's just their way of not dealing with the reality of Joseph. Why should they have to deal with a kid who makes funny noises and whose body moves so uncontrollably sometimes."

Dr. Smith stood placing his caring hand on Arianna's shoulder. "I can see why you hide your feelings." Tears fell on Arianna's cheek.

"There is one person I can't hide from." The good Doctor gave Arianna a tissue.

"Who can't you hide from?" As Arianna wiped her tears away, she said "Jesus, he knows everything." The Doctor was surprised with the answer he received.

"Jesus you say?"

"Jesus knows everything in my heart-every thought, even the scary ones. I have no one to be close with so at least I have him."

"I can appreciate your faith, but what about people?"

Arianna took a deep breath. "People, you say. All the people I love or trust are dead; seems since Jack's illness or Joseph's learning problems, friends and yes, even family have strayed. They just cannot understand."

"Now I understand. Arianna you need to go away."

"Go away, what do you mean?"

"You and the family need a break from everything. You especially need to heal."

Arianna reached for her purse and proceeded to pay the bill.

"Please try to get away."

As Arianna left the office she thought about England. England would be nice but it's just a dream.

That night when Jack came home, Jack asked what Dr. Smith said, while giving his wife a hug.

"I am much better."

Jack sighed. "Oh thank God."

"Listen Jack, Dr. Smith said he would like us to take a vacation." Jack pulled away.

"We'll see Arianna. You know I can't get out of work so easily."

Arianna's shoulders tightened.

"Jack, whether you like it or not, it's not in your hands. It's what I need right now that counts!"

Jack went to the kitchen for a glass of water.

"I'm sorry but this is all I can do for now."

Arianna was now fuming.

In twenty years of marriage she never hurt so much.

"You know Jack, when you need your treatments I am here. When Joseph has to go to his doctor and social worker there's no "We'll see!" There's no WE'LL SEE WITH THIS LADY! But with you, YOU CAN'T FATHOM THE TRUTH IF IT WERE PUT ON YOUR FACE WITH PLASTIC SURGERY! I'll never understand you Jack."

Arianna stormed into the bedroom and came out with Jack's pillow. She threw it at him. "WE'LL SEE, HOW'S THAT!!"

The next day Jack awoke with the biggest back and headache his body could ever handle. Arianna came in the kitchen, got a cup of coffee and said nothing. She went about her morning as usual, getting the kids up and ready for school.

That day, Jack's aching body was a reminder of what transpired last night. During lunch all he could think about was in twenty years of marriage his wife had never kicked him out of bed. She never once took the attention for herself. This time was different.

Jack's thoughts were broken when Dennis came in showing off tickets to the Bahamas. Dennis was the complete opposite of Jack-he acted on impulse and took the consequences later. Two glorious weeks with Erin and the kids-he couldn't wait to get home and surprise her.

Two hours later Jack called Arianna. Jack was feeling guilty.

"I am so very sorry. Please be ready with the kids. We'll go to Donovan's for dinner."

Arianna was very surprised and suspicious.

At the dinner table Jack could only read animosity on Arianna's face. He knew this hurt had cut too deep. While they waited for their meals, Joseph was his usual hyperactive self, making Mommy embarrassed with all his animal noises. They were both hoping for some quiet.

"Listen Arianna, I called Dad and explained our situation. Dad said we could borrow the money to go away as long as it will make you well again."

Animosity turned to tears. Arianna's father-in-law was always good to her.

"Please, I would like to go to England."

Jack went to hold Arianna's hand, his answer, "Yes, we can."

"After school closes I have made arrangements with Frank. I am taking three weeks."

Alexis looked up from her soda. "Three weeks Daddy?"

"Yes honey, three weeks."

Jack poured a glass of wine for Arianna.

"I know it doesn't make up for the way I treated you, but can it be a start?"

Arianna's tears said it all. It was about time. Her dream of England was about to come true.

Chapter Three

JOURNEY TO JULY

School was coming to a close. Arianna was anxiously standing outside the school gates. Alexis came out first with big smiles. She made the honor roll again and is now in the eighth grade. Joseph on the other hand came running over.

"Mommy! Mommy!" Tears rolling down his face. Mom knew why. Joseph got left back, his learning problem had taken it's toll. This is why he will start in a new school in September, so he could get the desperate help he needs.

School was not his favorite place. He would rather skip school than battle it every day.

Alexis asked if she could go to the movies with her friends. Mom had other plans.

"Honey I really want to go shopping for our trip." Alexis was a little miffed.

July 6th was just two weeks away. Passports were ready. All of the new luggage was in the house. After the new clothes were selected and purchased all they needed was the plane.

Kennedy Airport was twenty minutes from their home in Glendale, Queens, New York.

Daybreak-Five A.M., July 6th. "THANK GOD" is all Arianna and Jack said to each other this very morning. By this evening they will be in London.

They arrived at Kennedy at Nine AM New York time, Three PM London standard time. Alexis and Joseph were so excited. They had never been on an airplane before.

The children were excited yet bored at the same time, what with the line for tickets waiting at the gate and then finally boarding the plane. Once on the plane, Joseph assessed "Dad, its nothing but a big bus with wings."

Alexis being thirteen had a more sophisticated opinion. "Joe, be quiet. Can't you see it's an airplane stupid?"

"Alexis, name calling is not necessary."

"Oh Dad."

"Say you are sorry."

Alexis grunted "Sorry Joe."

Arianna just took her seat next to Jack. She couldn't wait to see the place she had only read about. Her heart was racing; Jack was apprehensive as usual.

Upon arriving at London International Airport, the kids were quite tired. Standing on line at baggage claim Joseph went on and on about how the clouds looked from close up.

"Dad I can't believe how really big they are."

"Alexis the earth. It's so flat from up there."

"OK, OK Joseph." Ten-year-old boys are impressive that way. Alexis, well her sights were on getting out of the airport, more or less even going home. Thirteen year old girls think more about staying with their friends and boys of course, than spending time with mom and dad.

In the cab going to the hotel they passed Windsor Castle and Big Ben.

"Dear God, they are just so beautiful."

"They certainly are Mrs. Lawrence."

"Mr. Jenkins, thank you for such a beautiful tour."

"You are very welcome Mrs. Lawrence."

Arianna's books have now become reality. Her thoughts were of her mother, and how much her mom wanted to travel before she died.

The funniest thing for the children was that the driver was on the left side. Alexis surveyed that English people were just like New Yorkers and London looked just like Manhattan-tall buildings, long streets, traffic, etc.

When they arrived at the Dalton Hotel, two men, one named Martin, the Guest Director and one named Charles, the Concierge, both handsome and very British met and helped the Lawrence family settle in.

"Excuse me Charles, has the hotel made arrangements at a hospital for my treatments?"

Arianna just stood there, staring at the floral centerpiece on the desk, thinking to herself, "as much as I am in the land of my dreams, reality always knocks on my door. It's inevitable. There's no peace from it. It will always follow me."

She knew Jack needed his care, she knew Joseph needed more attention than most boys of ten need. Just for once, just once, could she not have it follow her? Could she leave it all behind and lock the door to it? Ten years is a long time dealing with all of this. (I love them both very much.)

That evening, the Lawrence family had dinner in the Dalton's main dining room. The room was beautiful. The walls were decorated with ivory paint with pink and red rose appliques. Each applique was framed in an arch with gold and white trimmed scones. Each scone carried a pink candle with tea roses surrounding the base for bracelet.

The carpet carried a rose design and the tables had pink and white tablecloths and napkins. All the tables carried a centerpiece and a crystal vase with pink and red roses. The chairs were lavish armchairs with red velvet upholstery. Roses are Arianna's favorite flowers.

"Mommy, I feel like we are in Cinderella's castle."

"I agree Alexis."

The waiters all wore black dinner suits, white ruffled shirts and black ties. When their waiter Robert approached them, Alexis's eyes lit up. A young man around twenty, with brown hair and blue eyes, fair of skin, and to Alexis, a beautiful smile. He took their order and left for the kitchen.

"Mom, I think he's cute. Don't you?"

Jack looked at his daughter quite strangely.

"Well Jack, it seems we have a young lady at our table."

"No, I still see a little girl."

Alexis pouted. Mommy then whispered in her ear. "I'm glad to see that you have good taste in young men." Alexis smiled.

Joseph was fidgeting as usual. "Mom when is dinner ready?"

During dinner a phone was brought to the table. It was Dr. William Marcus. He said Jack could go to St. John's Hospital Saturday morning for treatment.

Later, they took a walk through the streets of London. They stood outside St. Peter's Church and read the mass schedule. The Lawrence's were enthusiastic yet tired. Jet lag set in. It was time for bed.

Chapter Four

EXCALIBUR

The first week had passed so quickly. It was Saturday morning. Jack and Arianna were driven to the hospital. Alexis and Joseph stayed at the hotel with a nanny and plenty of time to play in the game room.

To pass the time Arianna brought the pictures of their first week. While Jack received his treatment they sorted through and placed them in an album. Both could not believe how beautiful the people of London were to them and of course the amazing historical sights, which befell their inquisitive minds. Arianna could not believe that she visited Westminster Abbey, stood in front of Tudor Palace and actually watched the Queen and her Motorcade pass their hotel. Later that same day she watched the changing of the Queens Guards- their disciplinary drill was even quite impressive to the children.

Arianna felt so deeply honored to go to Southampton. She stood on the exact dock where Titanic sailed on that April 10, 1912 day. It was quite a haunting experience, especially because of her love and admiration for Titanic.

During this time, Arianna told Jack that after church on Sunday she wished to go horseback riding. She had mentioned it during the week but it seems that in between sightseeing they had other plans.

"I don't think this is a good idea Ari. It is not good for your back!"

Dr. Marcus came in to check on Jack's I.V.

"Please Dr. Marcus tell Ari that horseback riding is not a good idea for someone with a bad back."

Arianna was not to be reckoned with. Nothing will stop her. Her mind was set.

Sunday morning came. Arianna had arranged for her transportation. It would take an hour or so to travel to the Warwick Riding Academy in Westminster. This is where Camelot was built supposedly.

Jack and the children were not interested. They stayed behind. Arianna said she would return around five.

Coming up the causeway the Academy became quite visible. It was not as Arianna perceived it, but a quaint little cottage with a large barn attached to it. The receptionist asked if Arianna was an experienced rider. Arianna was-as a girl she rode all the time. One stipulation-she had to change from street clothes into a riding costume. Arianna was all too happy to comply. She had never worn one before.

Now in riding gear, Arianna felt wonderful. Special is more like it. The director of the Academy, Mrs. Dorothy Winters was pleased to see how Arianna took to the costume. She said it was as though Arianna was a natural horsewoman. It was time to meet her horse. His name is Sir Brach. Arianna thought how quaint that all the horses had names of Knights. This horse was an amazing beast. He was tall and muscular of body, with a brown mahogany coat, a long black mane and tail and a white star in between two beautiful ebony eyes. He was definitely a knight's horse and he was hers for the day.

Her riding companion and guide was Dorothy's husband Edmund Winters. A tall man of light olive complexion, medium build with silver blue eyes, dark gray hair growing white in the temples, with more white strands highlighting his thick massive hair. His face carried some age lines showing he was a man of some maturity. For some reason Arianna thought if she was a little older she could be attracted to him. Edmund helped Arianna saddle up and they were on their way.

Now, riding down the causeway, Edmund took out a map so that Arianna and he could plan their course together. The landscape was beautiful. The blue sky above. Green of every shade. Hills, valleys, and tall trees. You would think you could climb to get into Heaven's door. It was miraculous. For the first time in ten years Arianna felt human again.

Edmund told Arianna about the countryside. The conversation went back and forth about Jack and the children and Edmund spoke of his wife Dorothy and the horses they raise, but most of all the history of this land. Camelot and the tyranny of bloodshed that soaked such a beautiful land so many years before. To look now, who would believe such battles existed here!

They were about a mile away from the Academy when Edmund said "Mrs. Lawrence, I suggest we take the Blue route on the tour."

"Why is that Mr. Winters?"

"I sense by our conversation about Camelot that you would be interested in the ruins of Camelot."

"Oh I would Mr. Winters. Who knows, maybe we'll see some Knights or Dragons."

"Maybe!"

As they road on further--"My goodness what is this?"

"Mrs. Lawrence this is MERLIN'S POND named after the sorcerer who received..."

"I know, Excalibur--from the LADY OF THE LAKE, Merlin's Aunt."

"I am impressed Mrs. Lawrence."

"I know my legends Mr. Winters."

The lake was a beautiful azure as though the sky kissed it with color. In the middle of the lake was a fountain. It was made of gold and white marble shaped in an open seashell with The Lady of the Lake giving Merlin, Excalibur. Arianna could not believe what stood in front of her. It was as though every book she ever read had now come to life before her very eyes. Yet there was a sadness about Arianna and Edmund sensed it. He had seen it before with other people, but this one was different. Arianna's eyes gave her away. There was so much pain in those eyes. He only knew Arianna one hour and he could only imagine what might have hurt this beautiful lady.

As they approached the lake, Edmund realized he had forgotten the picnic lunch that came with the tour.

"Mrs. Lawrence?"

"Yes, Mr. Winters."

"I have to apologize."

"For what?"

"I have forgotten our lunch hamper."

"You did?" Arianna laughed, "I thought I had a short term memory sometimes!"

"Would you like to ride back with me?"

"Not really Mr. Winters, I could use sometime alone in this place of beauty."

"Well then, in your saddle bag there is a canteen and a book about this land. It will help enlighten your knowledge about legends."

Arianna reached in her saddlebag. "The Myths and Reality about Westminster."

"Oh, thank you Mr. Winters."

"Enjoy them and I'll return shortly."

Arianna watched Edmund mount his horse, then said, "Take your time."

Edmund rode away and all Arianna could think about was how silly Jack and the kids were. They could be enjoying nature and God's world with her, but computers and computer games were much more enticing. She took out her mini cam and started videotaping all this wonder. She thought to herself "When the world at home would come down on her she could put the tape in the VCR and remember this forever. It was now her private place, perhaps a gift from God.

Standing at the lake she saw her reflection in the water. How very strange she looked in her riding costume. Here stood this forty-year-old, five foot, two inch full figure of a woman. In a red jacket, black pants and a black P- cap and black chin high boots. There was a bridge, which led to the fountain. There was a sign on the bridge, actually it was a poem:

SEE
THE LADY OF THE LAKE
THROW A PENCE AND
MAKE HER WAKE
MAKE A WISH
WISH IT WELL
MAYBE MERLIN
WILL CAST A SPELL!!

Arianna laughed a kind of crazy laugh .She thought the whole thing a joke. Then walked across the bridge, looked at the fountain and made her way back under a tree to read, putting her camcorder down.

Arianna looked at her horse, Sir Brach. "You know Sir Brach, if I could wake The Lady of the Lake, I'd have a few choice words to ask her. Such as why my life is always so messed up?" For some reason, the lake made some funny bubbly noises. Sir Brach snorted as though he understood. "What was that?" Arianna spied the lake. "Must be some school of fish in there. Whatever."

Arianna was just annoyed that Jack and the kids weren't there. This would have been fun, a remembrance. She was feeling guilty as usual. Arianna sat herself down on a tree stump. She started skimming through the book Edmund told her to read. For some reason Sir Brach started snorting again. She turned a deaf ear. Arianna read the book and nervously started digging her heels in the soil. She felt her heels dig into something hard. At first she thought it was a tree root so she didn't pay any attention to it. But curiosity caught her. She looked down into the hole. What she saw was a piece of silver. Arianna thought, "Why should a piece of metal be buried out here in the forest?" She picked up a stick and started digging. The metal kept getting bigger. Sir Brach for some reason started acting funny, almost as though a warning.

After pursuing her dig, to her amazement, she lifted a sword, a magnificent sword, from the ground. She brought it to the lake and again Sir Brach made those snorting sounds. Arianna looked up quite annoyed, "HUSH UP YOU!" When the dirt was finally washed away Arianna examined the sword. She nervously kept talking out loud to Sir Brach. "Do you realize how old this must be? Who knows when this was buried here! I'm surprised it survived after all these years, it should have rusted."

As she examined it more closely, she noticed the pommel had a gold filigree design on it. In the middle of the design was a dragon wearing a crown holding a gold cross with two silver crossed swords on it. There were gold and silver leaves inlaid on the hilt. Within the body of the hilt was a red stone in the shape of a heart. On the tang were inscribed these words: TAKE ME, CAST ME. Arianna wondered what meaning could there be behind these words. The blade was a magnificent silver.

"This must have been the Knights crest. The house he came from. Well it serves Jack and the children right that they miss out on this adventure. Wait until I get back with this!"

"Hmm, I wonder what is taking Mr. Winters so long to get back. You know Sir Brach this thing is heavy." With all her might she swung the sword in a circle and up high in the air. To her amazement the sword sang. It was a piercing sound, as if two swords clashed and made the sound of a ringing bell, instead of metal. "DEAR GOD YOUR EXCALIBUR!! But, but you can't be." When she said her name again "EXCALIBUR?" the sword sang again as though she was happy to be in Arianna's presence. Being an amateur historian Arianna held EXCALIBUR in both hands and bowed to her. She knew deep in her heart she was in the presence of royalty, the greatest sword known to man. But how and why was she buried in the soil? According to her recollection of history Merlin threw Excalibur in the lake after King Arthur's death.

At that moment Edmund returned. He saw Arianna holding Excalibur. "Thank God! It is true, Excalibur does exist." He knew the journey had begun. He dismounted his horse, and walked towards Arianna.

"What do you mean by Thank God?"

"According to history only a Good man with a pure heart could be the guardian to Excalibur." All the while Edmund is staring anxiously at precious Excalibur.

"Well Mr. Winters I think this time she picked the wrong sex. Mr. Winters ONE simple question."

"What is that?"

Arianna's eyes kept examining Excalibur. "If Merlin threw Excalibur back in the lake, why was she buried in the soil?"

"I could only assess Mrs. Lawrence…"

"Please call me Arianna."

"And you call me Edmund." Both started walking back to their horses.

"Since the time of the Holy Wars, the people of Westminster scanned the lake for this very sword. When all failed they just thought Excalibur a myth, a legend to be spoken of in stories."

Arianna's gentle eyes looked up at Edmund. "May I hold Excalibur?" By all means please take her. Edmund embraced Excalibur as though seeing an old friend for the first time. "Edmund, I do believe you look better holding her than I. Just like a Knight in shining armor."

Arianna had gotten so carried away that when she came to her senses she remembered that she is a married woman with two children. The situation had gone too far. Her radiant smile vanished like a thief in the night. Arianna's cheeks were blushing. She changed the subject quickly.

"Edmund, we must return. I must show Jack and the children Excalibur." He was surprised with Arianna's change of heart.

"Then what?"

"Then what indeed!"

Edmund sensed confusion in Arianna. "Please Arianna, how did you know that this was Excalibur?"

Arianna's face seemed puzzled with the question. "Edmund, since I was a young woman I have always been fascinated with the Holy War stories. Can we either return or continue our journey?" Both mounted their horses. Edmund tied Excalibur to Sir Brach's saddlebag.

"Are we ready? Let's go!"

"History has always been my favorite subject. My father would think of me more a boy than a girl because of my love for horses, ships and swords." With these words her eyes filled with pain again, a distant stare shrouded them.

"Arianna, would you be willing to go on a quest?"

Arianna looked curious. "A quest? What kind of quest are you suggesting?"

Edmund directed his horse up the trail. Sir Brach followed. "Legend has it that the one who finds Excalibur should return her to her rightful owner." Arianna's curiosity heightened.

"Her rightful owner? You must be joking. All her rightful owners are dead. They are GHOSTS. Excalibur belongs in a museum."

"You do not understand Arianna. Merlin gave Excalibur back to The Lady of the Lake in anger."

"What you do not understand Edmund is that I cannot go anywhere! I must return." At that moment Edmund grabbed Arianna's arm, trying to reason with her. Tears filled her eyes and with every ounce of her being she wanted to run, run anywhere. Deep inside she wished to kiss Edmund and never return. Never return to pain and unending responsibility. Fear rushed in and Arianna thought Edmund to be crazed. All she could think about was how Jack didn't want to come here and how out of defiance she ventured alone.

In a flash she kicked Sir Brach and had that horse in a gallop of his life. She could feel the pain in her back start. Pain or no she must keep going. Thoughts rushed in as to how crazy Edmund is. Could he have raped me? Why did I ever come here? How can I explain all this to Jack? I can see it now-Jack's temper flying off the deep end. Well, maybe for once he will defend me and not think of himself.

"MY LORD, WHAT WAS EDMUND THINKING? A QUEST? A QUEST?"

Chapter Five

KING ARTHUR

Brach came to a quick halt, kicking and snorting. His ears twitching. Arianna looked around realizing Edmund was gone, nowhere in sight. She looked down the hill sighting the Riding Academy. Her heart started racing. She pulled on the bridal and led Sir Brach up the hill. Brach's body was now one with Arianna's. She could feel his body expand and contract with every breath and fearful heartbeat they both shared. All she wished to do was think, think of how to get back and how to get to a phone to call Jack.

Brach started those snorting sounds again. His ears kept twitching nervously.

"Sir Brach are those noises necessary, I am trying to think. Oh dear, is Excalibur with us? Oh thank God she's where Edmund tied her." Relieved to know Excalibur was there, Arianna continued. As soon as they reached the top of the hill both horse and rider were startled by what looked like a man dressed in a suit of armor sitting on a horse. To Arianna, more like a man dressed in a masquerade costume on his way to the ball.

"Halt stranger, you may go no further."

Arianna laughed and then panicked. Composing herself, all she could think of was who was this idiot and what does he want. But panic soon set in when another man dressed in the same way showed up behind her, sword drawn.

In a demanding voice he said, "DISMOUNT YOUR HORSE!" Both Sir Brach and Arianna tried to escape, but to no avail. The strangely dressed man pulled her off her horse and onto his. The other tied her hands and roped Sir Brach. She was now their prisoner and very afraid to speak. Her heart was racing so fast she could hardly breath. She was so afraid that all she could think of were Alexis and Joseph. If these men would kill her what would their lives be like? At that moment she gathered some strength.

"Who are you and what do you want with me?" Silence was her answer. Silence, except for Sir Brach's snorting and the sound of the men's armor hitting the saddles of their horses. Arianna noticed that the air changed, it was cool instead of warm.

As they came to the bottom of the hill the lake drew closer. Arianna started thinking, "if I could break free, maybe I can follow the trail. I'd be happy to find Edmund at this point."

The next sight she saw was a city. A city made of tan and white stone. As they entered the city Arianna noticed a crest hung on both columns. The crest was that of a wooden cross with two gold crossed swords and a crown surrounding them. Suddenly Excalibur sang. Arianna looked around, her mind rushing in all directions. In desperation she tried to loosen the strangers grasp on her, but to no avail. He held tighter and said nothing. A nervous laughter emerged and "Camelot" came flying forth from Arianna's mouth. Sir Brach snorted as though acknowledging her.

Riding further into the city, people were now looking at her. One woman dressed in another costume cried out, "what a strange looking man."

Arianna kept silent, thinking to herself "I am not a man." Then she realized "I am, in this ridiculous riding suit and my hair is hidden in this hat." Her nervous thoughts let her remember a line from a famous movie.

"Toto, I don't think we're in Kansas anymore."

In a blind rage, Arianna tried to break free, but this man was strong and held her tighter. Feeling very angry, and the loss of her freedom, Arianna kicked him, breaking the scary silence. "Laddie, you will pay for that later."

"Later? Where are you taking me?"

The other man simply responded, "You have a strange voice for a young man. Have some respect. Do you not realize that you are in the presence of the Kings Guards?"

Arianna tried to turn her head to look in this man's eyes but found herself too restrained. "You must be joking! Kings Guards. Indeed--WHERE THE HELL AM I?"

The horses kicked up a faster gallop. Arianna's heart was pounding harder in her chest. All that kept her sanity were thoughts of Alexis and Joseph. As much as her children could drive her crazy, this day they brought her sanity and some peace until she knew where the hell she was!

They stopped at a gate, a tall one, the size of a four-story building, held by tan stone columns the size of a five-story building. Fear ran through Arianna, fear she never felt before. A man on the other side of the gate yelled "LIFT!" With the command, the sound of chains rang through the air.

The three rode through. Sir Brach riding behind and Excalibur tied fast. They reached what looked like the main door of what appeared to be a castle. Arianna would not allow herself to stray. Concentrating on Jack, Alexis and Joseph were her directives. "Please God, what am I doing here? Please Jesus, I need your help. I am lost."

The guard dismounted his horse taking Arianna with him, pushing her through the doors, which were guarded by two men dressed as the others.

One of the guards told a young boy to tend to the horses. Walking through the halls, Arianna noticed a crest on the wall over another huge door. The crest was the same as on the sword she had just unearthed. Inscribed in gold lettering under the crest was one word: EXCALIBUR. One question Arianna asked herself, "How can this be?"

Two guards opened the doors and as Arianna was escorted in she could spy at least fifty people in court, all looking, all shouting "HE'S A WITCH, A SPELL!! The king will have you burned!"

Arianna held fast. Her hands were shaking through tightening ropes. Her legs were so shaky she fought to stand. One man with tall sandy hair and piercing brown eyes made circles around her.

"Sire, what manner of dress is this?"

Another came right up to her face – "Sire, what witchery has brought this young man? We should question him."

Arianna's eyes scanned the room for anything sane. She thought herself in a dream. "If only I can awaken, this will all be gone."

Then out from the crowd came a tall man around six feet two inches tall in height, medium frame, with long dark brown hair with streaks of silver running through it.

His skin was light but tanned. He wore a long sleeve gray shirt, gray leggings and black chin high boots. Completing his attire was a long tunic of black and blue, with a dragon on the breastplate. He had a walk only a king would have. Very commanding.

As this striking man approached, Arianna could only let herself think, "Could this be King Arthur, this cannot be Tintagel Castle?" She answered herself quickly. "You must be joking, this is 1998 not 525 AD. He is dead you fool."

This man now stood one foot in front of her. His eyes were piercing blue. His face wore the lines of a man who's life toiled too tiresome for him. As he looked in Arianna's brown eyes, he could almost look into her soul. This disturbed him.

Arianna gathered the strength to ask, "May I speak?"

The court shouted, "How dare he speak!"

Again she dared, "May I assume…"

Arthur beckoned with his hand for quiet. "Speak young man, what do you seek?"

"Am I in the presence of King Arthur Pendragon?"

"How do you know of him?" asked this striking man.

Arianna's eyes and Arthur's eyes followed each other's.

"I have heard about your kindness Sire, and how you rule your kingdom with fairness of heart and soul." Fear rushed through Arianna's body. She begged, "Please tell me you are he."

This King stood before her completely perplexed with this stranger. He folded his arms and stroked his beard. He then walked over, placed his hand on Arianna's shoulder and replied "I AM HE."

With all her strength, Arianna knelt before King Arthur. While rising to her feet the crowd roared. "Be careful Sire, you could be brought under the same spell."

Arianna scanned the room for Excalibur. "Could she be on the Round Table, maybe hanging on the wall? No, there by King Arthur's chair." She was nowhere in sight. Her carpal tunnel was now aching from the ropes.

King Arthur asked "Young man, where do you come from?"

Arianna watched Arthur work the floor.

"I come from far away, Sire."

"What manner of garment is this?"

"The way we dress in my home."

"Home, where is home?"

Arianna thought carefully. She replied "New Amsterdam, Sire. It is on the other side of the ocean."

The court screamed "Sire, this means war. You realize this!"

"I come in peace, my King. I mean no harm to anyone! I am only a traveler", trying to break free from the ropes. "Please understand this."

King Arthur looked so confused. He looked at Arianna with so many questions on his face.

"Your Majesty may I speak again?"

A man cautioned Arthur "Be careful Sire, it might be some trickery."

"Sir Gawain I will hear this young man."

"My Lord." With these words Arianna knelt again. "Is there a man among you named Merlin?" Arianna scanned the room again hoping someone would come forward. Again the crowd cautioned.

Arthur signaled quiet with his hand. "How do you know of Merlin?"

"I have heard about him in my travels Sir Gawain, that is all."

Arianna's head was starting to feel dizzy, the way she felt before she became ill. She kept telling herself "STAND TALL WOMAN, STAND TALL FOR GOD'S SAKE. DON'T FALL!"

One of King Arthur's men came forward.

"Sire, please. If this young man comes in peace, find out why he is here."

King Arthur shook his head in agreement.

"What is your name?"

As Arianna tried to speak her voice became hoarse. "My name is Ari, My Lord." Arthur paced the floor again.

"Why are you here?" Arianna stiffened her legs. Her stomach and throat tightened. King Arthur and Arianna's eyes met frozen together.

"My Lord I found your sword. I-I found Excalibur." Arthur's face was shocked.

"This cannot be."

"But it is. She is tied to my horse."

"William, to the stables."

"Right away, Sire." Arthur himself fled to his chambers in search for Excalibur.

Arianna stood frozen in time while William and Arthur searched for the precious sword. As the knight entered court with Excalibur I, and King Arthur entered court with Excalibur II, both swords sang with the ring of Church bells in celebration, the celebration of a wedding, a union. These men at court shut their ears. Arianna and Arthur could not believe theirs. In the confusion of it all a man stepped out of the crowd. Arianna noticed a man dressed in a long brown cloak, his head covered with a hood. He was carrying a gold sword.

Arianna did not pay attention as to who the man could be. All she saw were two swords, one old looking and one shining with sunlight. Sir William could hardly hold Excalibur I. Her song was so full of life. While giving the sword to Arthur, both sang their song in unison.

Arianna broke down. Her tears ran. This vision was too overwhelming to contain oneself.

Arthur's men moved to surround him, leaving Arianna unguarded. The stranger dressed in brown made his presence known to Arianna. He stepped out of the crowd. Arianna watched this stranger come closer to her. She was astonished to see... Edmund?

"I am Merlin," he said.

She replied "You are Edmund! YOU can't be Merlin! You look and speak like a man named Edmund. But you can't be he or be here either, can you? For that matter how am I here?"

The confusion continued with both swords' songs starting to calm themselves. Merlin replied, "I am Merlin and Edmund. Listen quickly. The ages have sent you to right a wrong I made in this time. I was made to search for you by my aunt, The Lady of the Lake, years ago."

"What? I-I do not understand."

"Hush now." Arthur comes forward holding both swords. As Arthur approached Arianna, Merlin stepped aside.

"Ari."

"My Lord."

"Do you know who this man is?"

"My Lord, this is Merlin."

The court cautioned as Sir Fredrick looked straight at Arianna.

"WARLOCK!!"

Arianna cringed. The word frightened her.

"Ari, how are there two Excalibur's?"

Arianna looked at Arthur. "I do not know My LORD, I DO NOT KNOW."

Merlin than waved his hand and asked Arthur, "Do you trust my judgement?"

Arthur replied "Indeed I do."

Merlin then took Excalibur I from Arthur and cut the ties on Arianna's hands. Again shouts. Arthur again calms them.

"Again I ask Arthur, Do you trust me?"

"Since I was a babe in your arms I have trusted you as no other."

Merlin stepped in front of Arianna. Her eyes were trusting and fearful at the same glance. Her hands were in so much pain at this point.

"Arthur must know you are a woman."

Her wounded hands shaking, Merlin proceeded to remove Arianna's hat. He saw more pain than he could have imagined coming deep from her eyes--her soul. He saw faint images of a hard past.

He whispered "I am sorry. Trust me, I implore you."

Arianna was so confused, maybe even dazed. This trail was taking its toll.

He then pulled the pins from her hair, allowing her beautiful long brown hair to cascade down her back.

"A WOMAN," they shouted! "BY WHAT TRICKERY!!"

Merlin grabbed Arianna's hands. "Hold on, nothing will happen to you."

Pulling away in total fear, Arianna said: "Now they will really think I am a witch."

"You must trust me." Her hands were shaking so uncontrollably.

"Why did you not help me earlier?"

"I had to know for sure that you are pure of heart."

Arthur, still trying to quiet the crowd, took Excalibur II and raised her high. Her song sang again. The song quieted the crowd to a soft hush.

Standing in front of Arianna, King Arthur examined her body from head to foot. He then reached to caress Arianna's hair. He realized the streaks of gray in her hair showed that she was a woman of maturity. She pulled away in fear. With his assuring voice he said: "I will not harm you."

Arianna felt herself melt as this strikingly handsome man asked, "What is your real name?"

"My real name is Arianna Lawrence, My Lord."

"What a beautiful name." He then held Arianna's face with both hands, looking deep in her heart. He saw only a beautiful woman. He then took her hand and caressed the wounds the ropes made and kissed them.

With the knowledge of a true King, he took Excalibur I from Merlin's hand and gave her to Arianna. Excalibur sang softly in her careful hands.

Arthur knew there was something special about this strange woman. He then kissed her on both cheeks as though a long lost daughter and declared: "This is Lady Arianna Lawrence. You are to treat her with nobility and respect. This is my law today and always."

"Sire, do you know what you are doing?"

Anger was written on Arthur's face. "I do Gawain, I do"

He then took Arianna by the hand and beckoned Merlin and he to leave the room.

There was such a quiet in court as the three left.

Chapter Six

KINGS' CHAMBERS

Walking through the great halls the walls felt larger than life. The decor was of stained glass, stone columns at least twelve feet high and four feet in diameter. Drapes of red and gold hung over the main windows. The hall felt a mile long, a lit up path with no end in sight. There was at the end a staircase. The three climbed and at the top, two cherry wood doors set in an arch frame. Each door was adorned by a cross carved in the wood with a pair of silver swords crossed over each. A young man guarded each door. Both dressed as the others but neither wore a sword or crest. Dutifully the boys stood at attention as they opened the doors. Arianna realized that this is the kings' chamber.

King Arthur offered Arianna a comfortable chair, then ordered Daniel, one of the young men, to get her some food and drink.

The chair felt like a long lost friend. At this point nothing, not even the kings' chambers, impressed Arianna. All she wanted was to rest. Merlin soaked a cloth with cool water so Arianna could take care of her wounds.

Something did catch her eye. On the table was a brass plate and on it were two wedding rings, almost a shrine. It prompted Arianna to play with her own wedding ring. This made her wonder how Jack and the children were. She was so far away. Will she ever see them again?

Young Daniel returned with a tray of mutton, bread and a chalice of red wine. The food was good but the wine went to Arianna's tired mind. She fell asleep in the chair.

All the while Merlin is trying to explain all this to Arthur. King Arthur had a rare gift. He knew how to listen as a friend and father at the same time. But today he listened to Merlin with an open mind and as a son to a father. He tried to understand that whatever happened at the lake or in the forest could have been one of Merlin's eccentric stories he made to teach him a lesson or a vision, sometimes a frightening one, into the future. Usually Merlin's visions were real and Arthur would always heed to their wisdom.

Arthur watched this rare woman sleep. He stroked her cheek and wondered who she was, and why did God or the devil send her to him. Inside he knew Merlin was only explaining in half-truths.

Merlin stepped outside on the verandah. He was haunted by what he saw in Arianna's eyes. Arthur followed. He saw something in his good friend's face he had never seen before. Dejection was written on this man's face. He was disturbed by this part of Merlin he was now privy too. Merlin was always a serious man, but he always had a humorous side.

Arthur looked back in chambers and saw Arianna sleeping. He thought, "how on earth could there be two swords?" There was such a silence between these two men.

Arthur returned to chambers to sit at his desk writing the days events in his tablet. An hour past, Merlin stood outside watching dusk come in and the oppression it can sometimes bring.

Arthur was never at a loss for words but this night cast a strange spell. Here, an old friend whom he admired as a father and thought he knew, was a stranger and this strange woman seemed more a friend than a stranger!

Arthur again watched as his comrade, his guide in life suffered through lighting the lamp on the table. He poured a chalice of wine, picked up the chalice, sniffed the sweet aroma and sipped it. As he swallowed this aphrodisiac, the silence broke.

Merlin put the chalice down and picked up both swords. He saw the reflection of a man he did not know any longer.

"Arthur, I have failed."

Arthur looked curious.

"I made a promise to myself when I was a lad, that I would never hurt anyone as my mother Queen Mab did. I made a promise that I would never use my magic for my own advantage. Yet today I broke all promises to myself." Merlin then takes another sip of wine.

"This woman does not belong here. The pain she has had in her lifetime has been enough to bear. I did not have to give her more."

His confession was interrupted when Sir Ralph came in.

"Ralph, what is it?"

"It is Modred, Sire. He is threatening the North Villages."

"What does he want?"

"Modred said that if they do not provide himself and his men with half the winter provisions, he will burn their villages and rape their women."

Arthur places his elbows on the table, putting his hands together as if in prayer. He cradles his forehead on the fold and shakes his head repeatedly, saying, "Dear God, what have I brought into this world? My hope for peace continues to elude me." Arthur folds his arms.

"Modred takes pleasure in threats to women and children. My son knows how to make me feel as though I have failed him, failed my people. Arthur shakes his head and takes an exhausting breath. I have given everything I can to him and Camelot and yet he takes the last drop I have."

"He knows I love him, he is my son."

Arianna started to awaken at this time. She kept quiet so she could hear Arthur.

"Modred may be your son Sire, but he has no place on the throne."

"Arthur's eyes were angry yet understanding."

"Yes Ralph, I know."

"If Modred became King, Camelot and England would all become enslaved to his every whim. He should perish in battle before we see such a time."

"I agree Merlin."

Out of the disparity came Arianna's waking voice.

"My Lord Arthur, I know about sons who bring nothing but grief to your heart."

"My LORD, has she been here all this time?"

"She has, Ralph."

25

"Can she be trusted? We know nothing about her." Arthur nervously played with a stick.

"Ralph, do I have a good judge of character?"

"A very good judge, Sire."

"You do know that I help people who are in need of help?"

Ralph stood baffled by the interrogation and answered, "All the time Sire."

"Then look in Lady Arianna's eyes. See her gentleness. There is not any hate or malice. She is a guest in my home and here she will stay."

Ralph bowed his head, "Your will be done My Lord."

"Ralph, tell John and Percy that I will meet them in chapel to discuss this urgency. MODRED MUST BE STOPPED!!"

With his orders at hand, Ralph left the room in haste.

Arthur stepped away from the table, took one look at Arianna--- shaking his head in dismay. "Dear God Merlin, tell Lady Catherine to help Lady Arianna into some decent clothes. Tell her to use Guenevere's wardrobe. At least they will be put to good use."

Then he fled the room.

"Daniel."

"Yes, Merlin?"

"Please tell Lady Catherine to meet Lady Arianna and myself in Queen Guenevere's room."

"Right away, My Lord."

Chapter Seven

MERLIN AND ARIANNA

"Why did you run away?"

"You terrified me."

Arianna put another cool cloth on her rope burns.

"I do not understand."

"I was carried away with Excalibur and you that somewhere in my heart I really did want to go on a quest. I was terrified, terrified with the feelings I felt at that very moment."

"What feelings?"

Merlin went to touch Arianna's arm. She pulled away.

"Dear God, I understand."

"Do you Merlin? I was afraid I would be an Adulterer. I am married, you are married. I have not had such feelings for anything or anyone as I did by that lake in a long time. They scared me." Merlin paced the room.

"You could have tried to trust me."

Arianna threw the cloth at Merlin.

"Trust you, Merlin? I knew a man named Edmund out there. I knew this man for only an hour! I was afraid I would go on a quest and never wish to return! Even though I did not know what that quest was."

"I understand now."

"Why did you not call yourself by your real name, Merlin?"

" Do you not think people would be a little suspicious of a man named Merlin?" Merlin stands over Arianna, stroking Arianna on the cheek in a fatherly kind of way. Arianna realizes he is a kind and gentle man. She now recognizes that his eyes carry the same pain she so gravely feels. She tells herself "Help him." She takes a deep breath.

"Your Aunt, The Lady of the Lake sent you looking for me or someone like me?"

For reasons of being tired they both broke out in a delirious kind of laughter.

"She certainly did, Lady Arianna."

"Please, that title, am I really in Camelot?"

"Let us get you into some decent clothes."

"Did I really meet King Arthur?"

"You did."

"How?"

"As I said, Excalibur seeks out the hands of someone with a pure heart and soul."

"I am far from that person." There's a chill in the room and Merlin drapes his cloak on Arianna.

"No Arianna, Excalibur knows who you are, faults and all. That is why she knew you would find her someday."

"But how am I here?"

"Your heart brought you here."

"My heart?"

Merlin takes Arianna's hand in his. "Your heart and your belief in Camelot."

Merlin's eyes take on a distant stare.

"I made a mistake by throwing Excalibur back in the lake. I was angry. My Aunt told me I had to search for someone with a good heart to help me correct my mistake. Somehow My Lady, I think, The Lady of the Lake brought us both together. I do not know how or why either."

"Merlin, do not say another word." Arianna puts her forefinger on Merlin's lips.

"SHH, SHH -We will both help each other. Can I assume we are close to the fatal battle which has brought me here?"

"You do know your history."

"Then we know we cannot change history but we can help it. Then we will do that when the time comes."

Merlin's eyes fill with tears. "Let's find the strength, Merlin, to do whatever God or magic wills."

Merlin takes Arianna's hand, opens the door and they both walk the great halls together.

Chapter Eight

THE QUEENS' ROOM

"Merlin, I do not think you belong here."

Lady Catherine, a woman around Arianna's age, is waiting patiently by the door. Her examining eyes give Arianna a quivery feeling.

"My Lady, I wish to sit here and secure Lady Arianna's safety."

"Lady Arianna, how strange to hear that."

"What do you mean?" Merlin gestures quiet to Arianna.

"What I mean is I never thought I would be called Lady."

Lady Catherine laughed a cautious sort of laugh then asked, "Lady Arianna, why do you dress as a man?"

"Where I come from, it is easier to look like a man. Men seem to think women are play objects rather than human beings."

"It is a shame. You are a beautiful woman. You should wear beautiful clothes."

Arianna could not help but take in the room. Guenevere loved blue. The walls were yellow, and etched in the walls were beautiful birds and flowers. The bed had a sky blue cover with a white and gold satin dust ruffle. The windows were tall, about eight feet, set in an arch frame. The dressings were royal blue with the same white and gold ruffle. The chairs had blue and gold upholstery. There was a fireplace to the right side of the room. Arianna wished she could take the room home with her.

"Lady Catherine, are you related to King Arthur?"

"Catherine opened the wardrobe door. "I am unfortunately not, but my husband is Sir Gawain."

"Do you have children?"

"Yes, two, a boy fourteen years and a girl twelve years." Merlin clasps both hands behind his back.

"I do apologize My Ladies, I have neglected to introduce both of you."

Catherine moves over to Merlin, pats him on the back and says "Merlin, I believe your head to be in the stars most of the time."

"I believe you are right Catherine." Merlin's eyes and face smile boyishly.

"Lady Arianna, are you married?"

Arianna then moves over to the wardrobe, eyeing the beautiful clothes. "Yes I am. My husband is Jack Lawrence and I also have two children, a girl Alexis, thirteen years and a son Joseph, ten years."

Catherine takes Arianna's left hand in hers, saying, "Your wedding ring is beautiful, yet simple at the same time."

"Thank you, I do not like big heavy jewels. I do not put importance on such matters."

"This is a sign of nobility."

"Oh, Thank you."

Merlin was pleased with Arianna's response.

"Why are Guenevere's clothes still here? After all, she no longer lives here."

Catherine shrugs her shoulders. "I do not know. I guess Arthur never saw a need to get rid of them. My personal opinion, he should have burned them!"

"Please sit down on the chair while I prepare your clothes. King Arthur is not the kind of man to do something so irrational. He always feels something good can come out of many problems. Especially Galahad."

"Galahad?"

Arianna looks at the dresses on the bed. "Lancelot's son lives here?"

"Oh yes, Arianna."

"Merlin, I was not aware of this."

"I do not understand. I thought you knew about…" Arianna cuts his sentence.

"Merlin, people sometimes write only what they want you to know. The truth is never fully told."

"Then it is time you knew the truth."

"Merlin, I think it is time you left us alone. The King wished the Lady dressed properly, and I must go home to my family." Merlin stepped outside to the balcony. He placed himself near the door where he could listen.

"Lady Catherine these clothes are beautiful." Lady Catherine eyes Arianna's body.

"It is amazing, you and Guenevere are almost the same size and shape."

"Really? I did not know this."

As Catherine helped Arianna out of her clothes, she noticed a cross of gold on Arianna's neck.

"Do you follow Jesus? Are you a Christian?"

"I am a Christian."

"Do you know who Jesus is? Arianna knew the reason for the question. Arianna stood proud and answered the question.

"Jesus is the Son of God, Mary and the foster son of Joseph. He died on the cross for our sins. We owe everything to him." Arianna made the sign of the cross on herself. Catherine took a deep breath and a sigh of relief. She now knew that all was well with Arianna.

The red and gold dress was the garment of choice. Catherine prepared the dry sink so Arianna could wash up. Then she brushed and braided Arianna's long locks. Lady Catherine then helped Lady Arianna put the dress on.

"Well look at you. I knew there was a beautiful woman hiding there." Arianna felt as if she was transformed into a queen. Merlin knew by the sound of things that the ladies were ready. While walking in the room Merlin stopped short.

"My Lady you are a vision, a true beauty. Arthur will be pleased."

Arianna thought to herself, "Arthur will be pleased, What might Jack say? If there was some way he could see me? He certainly will not believe this story in a thousand years."

Arthur's voice resonated through the halls.

"GAWAIN! WILLIAM! And with one louder burst, MERLIN!!"

"Arianna, take Excalibur. Keep her safe."
"I have to go with you."
Arianna reached for Merlin's arm. "The hour of your need for me is at hand."

Again Arthur's voice shattered the halls. "MERLIN!"
The door burst open.
"I need you in the West Wing. NOW!" A chill ran up Merlin's spine. He could hear Arianna's words warning him. He also knew Arianna could not change the course of history.

"My Lord may I help you?" Arthur was surprised to see Arianna so beautifully transformed.

"You are a vision My Lady, and you as always Lady Catherine. Forgive the intrusion." Arthur scans the room remembering Guenevere, then looks at the two visions in front of him and being a gentleman says " My Ladies, if beauty could conquer Modred then you would be my shields. Modred dances with the devil and beauty will not be his downfall. HEAVEN'S ARMOR WILL BE!"

"We ask only that from God." Arthur takes Beautiful Excalibur from her sheath and holds her close to his heart.

"When I was a young man, Merlin brought me before Council, the Angles needed a King. He said that I had a good heart and a good sense for Leadership. He also reminded them that he was of Noble blood. My father was King Uther and my mother Lady Igraine. I should be allowed to enter the contest for Excalibur." Merlin then stands next to Arthur and places his hand on Excalibur with Arthur's.

"Yes, The Lady of the Lake told me that if Arthur had a good and faithful heart he would receive EXCALIBUR into his trust."

Arianna stood staring at King Arthur, listening to every word as though they were gospel.

"Excalibur was imbedded in a stone, a magic stone, made by the Lady and Merlin. Only the true and rightful King would be allowed Excalibur in his trusting hands. That day I stood at that stone, held Excalibur's hilt, and said a prayer. I asked God if I was worthy of such a title and the responsibilities and riches that come with it, please give me the heart to handle it. At that very moment Excalibur was drawn from the stone. In front of council I was declared King."

"I was so proud of him that day."
Arthur blushes. "Today I say the same prayer, with Excalibur at my chest. I ask for the heart and the wisdom to handle my son in whatever way God wills."

Sir Gawain entered the room. "Catherine, what are you doing here?"
Catherine walks over to Gawain and kisses his cheek.
"His Lordship asked if I could help Lady Arianna." Gawain looked at Arianna. "Well at least she looks like a woman."
"Gentlemen, we have disturbed the ladies enough. I apologize."
"Catherine, may I speak with you?" Catherine and Merlin speak privately in the hall.
"You look disturbed Merlin?"

"I am. Lady Arianna knows about our beautiful Camelot but she needs to know everything. Please stay a little longer and tell her."

"I do not understand."

"Please, you could help me greatly. It will help Arthur."

"Whatever you need Merlin."

"Thank you dear friend." Merlin kissed Catherine on the hand, then proceeded to The West Wing.

Chapter Nine

LADY CATHERINE AND LADY ARIANNA

"I thank you Lady Catherine for helping me."

"You are quite welcome."

"Please forgive Arthur for intruding as he did. Modred has him so bewildered these days. He is not the Arthur that Gawain and I once knew."

"I could very well understand how one life can change another."

"What do you mean?" Arianna steps over to the window looking out into the night.

"What I am trying to say is that since I have been married…"

"I know exactly what you are about to say. Marriage, children."

"No, not exactly. My son is sickly. He takes all I have to give some days. There are days when I feel as his Lordship feels."

"I am so sorry to here this." Catherine pours a chalice of wine for each of them.

"Please tell me about the King Arthur you and Gawain once knew."

"Come, we will sit outside and enjoy the evening sky." Arianna could not believe how the sky looked. God's black dome illuminated by such beautiful jewels.

"This is the sky Arthur loved. He and Merlin could sit for hours playing a game as to who could name more constellations. They would laugh and play." Catherine flutters her hands in front of her face.

"Oh, Arthur and Merlin were so good together." Her beautiful hazel eyes opened wide, her words filled with so much love.

"My goodness, Arthur and Gawain were such good looking men. Arthur tall, and so stately looking. Gawain, tall, quite good looking with those brown curls and brown eyes. Oh, let us not forget the strong chin. It is no wonder I fell in love with him. They could make me laugh." Arianna takes a sip of wine.

"Catherine, I fell in love with Jack for that same reason. Jack is still a good looking man."

"You know Arianna, I guess they all look good for old men." They both laughed together as schoolgirls do.

"Could I ask you why are you telling me all of this?"

"I get this feeling deep down Merlin wishes you to know. I know he trusts you. It is written in his eyes." Arianna takes a deep breath.

"Merlin trusts me. What an honor!"

"Lady Catherine, why does Modred hate Arthur so?"

"Oh dear Arianna, Arthur married a woman from Lyoness named Guenevere."

"How long ago?"

"Twenty-five years ago, give or take a few years."

"I see."

"She was around twenty years younger than he. They were so much in love. Arthur could not live without Guenevere. Arthur had a Knight whom he cherished very much: his name-Sir Lancelot. Arthur left for Rome to fight the Holy Wars leaving Lancelot in charge of Camelot. Arthur was away for at least six months. Guenevere and Lancelot found eyes for each other."

"Talk about a perfect situation."

"When Arthur returned, those roaming eyes betrayed themselves to Arthur."

"Arthur is an astute man."

"That he is, Arianna."

"Guenevere's cold heart drove Arthur into the arms of an old flame, The Lady Morgana. That unfortunately conceived Modred."

"Oh no, I thought he was Guenevere and Arthur's son."

"No, he could not be Guenevere's son. Guenevere was a barren woman."

"How is Galahad Lancelot's son?"

"During this time, Lancelot's father, Sir Ban of Britain betrothed him to The Lady Elaine of Astolate. Sir Ban called Lancelot home and he and Lady Elaine were married. Time and distance did not stop this affair. Lancelot returned. In the meantime, Guenevere found out about Morgana and Modred. She was jealous of Modred and paid Queen Mab nicely to escort them out of Camelot with a condition that she and the boy never return."

"A royal vixen, she was."

"That's putting it mildly. Guenevere was rich and spoiled. She knew how to get what she wanted. Lancelot was kept on as a Knight of the Round Table and Arthur tried to turn a blind eye. Sir Ban became ill, this meant Lancelot would have to return home to Astolate. This return brought the birth of Galahad. Ban died soon after Galahad's birth. Upon Lancelot's return, Arthur soon found Guenevere and Lancelot together. Arthur was gravely hurt. Guenevere and Lancelot were put on trial for collusion." Arianna got up to smell the roses.

"Please, do not remind me of a trial."

"Arianna, Arthur could have had both of them executed. Instead, he was merciful and banished them from Camelot. When Morgana found out Guenevere was no longer queen, she returned to Camelot."

"My God, His Majesty must have been shocked to learn about Modred." Catherine pulls a twig off the rose bush.

"No, not shocked. Hurt. You would think these thorns pierced his heart. She wanted money and for Modred to stay in Camelot. Arthur would have none of it."

"Was Modred really his son?"

"He did not know." Tears filled Arianna's eyes. "It seems as though Arthur's women raped him for his love and his crown." Catherine looked so strangely at Arianna.

"Dear God, I would never have put it that way, but it could very well be rape."

"After a time, Merlin helped Arthur accept Modred, but it was all too late. Mab had taken over Modred and Morgana."

"What about Galahad?"

"Lady Elaine and Lancelot's ill fated marriage and his banishment were too much for such a genteel, gentle woman. Illness befell her and she passed away." Arianna and Catherine moved back inside. It is getting cold and they warm themselves by the fire.

"My Lord Jesus, young Galahad without a mother."

"Not only that, not a home either. Lancelot's sin brought that child hardship. Elaine's family did not want him. Lancelot's cousin Edward informed Arthur and Arthur sent for Galahad." Arianna goes to warm her hands by the fire.

"Poor Galahad, the man who punished his father."

"No, Arianna, not Arthur so much. Modred. Modred made things hard for Galahad. Arthur would defend him. Therefore, Modred's hate for Arthur was ignited with the help of Queen Mab. Merlin tried so hard to stop Mab's Black Magic but the more Arthur and Merlin resisted her, the stronger Modred became, and the more insane he became. Modred came of age and therefore formed his own army."

"So, now this is where we stand."

"Exactly."

"Catherine, hopefully we will be strong enough to help Arthur take his stance against this madman."

From Arianna's room the ladies could hear the men arguing about how the battle should be against Modred.

"Come, Catherine, let us listen at the door." Catherine was not accustomed to this behavior.

"Come, let us find out what the men do when we women are not there."

"Let us go, Arianna. My curiosity has been fired up."

Chapter Ten

THE WEST WING

King Arthur began his caucus with a prayer while pacing the floor.

"Dear God, I ask for your guidance to fight my son, for you to care of my armies and their families. Please send your Angels to protect us in our endeavors. AMEN."

"What can you tell me, Ralph?"

"The northern regions are prosperous as are the north and southeastern villages. Sire, Modred knows of your riches and this is why he plans his war."

"My riches? I give my people free will. This is why they are prosperous. All I ask is that they are good to each other." Ralph draws his sword from its sheath, nervously rubbing his fingers over the blade.

"Modred's men spread vicious lies. He tells your people that you plan on taking half their harvest, keep it here and sell it to the merchants. Hence, become richer than you already are."

"Since Modred was a boy, he has tested every drop of my love and my patience. He has used my crown as his scapegoat and my people have suffered greatly."

"Lady Catherine." I heard and I came quickly.

"Galahad!" Arianna looked surprised.

"I have come to help Uncle Arthur."

"You are scarcely a man. Arthur needs strong men with experience of sword and shield to fight." Galahad folds his arms in front of him and with some dismay in his voice.

"I will be a man soon enough. I have to help him."

Arianna stood transfixed listening to this young man, completely amazed at Galahad. He stood at least six feet tall at eighteen years of age, having sandy brown hair and hazel blue eyes. He had broad shoulders and a straight body. He was a truly beautiful young man. Arianna wondered if Lancelot looked like this!

As Galahad peeked into the west wing, he finally took notice of Arianna.

"Why, you are the lady with the sword like Uncle Arthur's."

"I am she." He noticed it was tied to her apron. His eyes came out of their sockets. As most boys do, he went to touch Excalibur. Arianna pulled away.

"Young man, please, this is a King's sword. King Arthur and Merlin will not allow anyone to touch her."

"What else is new. Uncle Arthur will not let me polish his other sword. He says he takes pleasure in seeing her shine for him." Their conversation was interrupted when John entered the room.

"My Lord." John had despair written on him, his arm badly wounded.

"Modred has burned the village of Southampton. Women, children are all dead. Arthur sank in his chair. The expression on his face was that of being impaled. Galahad intrudes at the wrong time.

"My uncle, please, let me help you."

With these words, Arthur's face changed. He also noticed Lady Catherine and Lady Arianna outside the door.

Galahad knelt beside his heart-broken uncle. "Please, My Lord, let me fight by your side. You have given me so much, I love you."

Arthur placed his hand on Galahad's cheek while looking straight into his eyes.

"Thank you, but I need you here."

"Why? I could better help you in the fields."

"No, my son. You can serve me by helping watch over my people here. Lady Catherine, Lady Arianna you can come in now. Sir Gawain, come forward please."

Arthur took Gawain's hand and Catherine's hand then held them together.

"Gawain, my brother, my friend, guard my castle. Make sure it is here when I return."

"Lady Arianna."

"My Lord."

You are to stay here and watch Galahad. Right now he needs a mother. Something tells me you can give him guidance." Arianna bowed her head.

"It will be an honor and privilege, My Lord."

Arianna's eyes filled with tears. How could he know?

Chapter Eleven

THE ENDLESS DAY

Midnight approached and the night made way for preparing Arthur's armies. The caucuses went on discussing weapons, strategies and placement as if playing a game of chess-Rook to King four and so on until checkmate.

Wives are preparing their hearts to say good-bye, hoping they will see their spouses and sons again.

The sun shone an unfriendly face. As news traveled about Southampton, grief filled the villages.

"Peter."

"My Lord."

"Ask Sir Gawain to meet me in my private courtyard."

"Right away My Lord." Peter ran through the castle with the message.

A few minutes later.

"My Lord, you sent for me?"

"Gawain, I am not as young as I used to be. My sword and shield have been silent for a while now. Can we...?

"Say no more my king." Gawain drew his sword and together the exercise began. As King and Knight fenced together, they spoke of the past. They spoke of the Holy Wars.

"How could the Holy Grail have eluded them?"

"I do not know Gawain, I do not know. Remember when we were young, the swords clashing and ringing through words of friends."

Together they shouted, "THEY WERE OURS TO COMMAND!!"

Through the thunder of swords it was a beautiful tribute to these two men. Catherine laughs as she peers through the galley window.

"Oh it is good to see Arthur laugh. Look Arianna, they pretend each is the enemy only in a "Tom Foolery" kind of way." Arianna cradled her face in both hands. As she watched Arthur's swordplay she found herself consumed by his gentle majesty.

"I know what you are thinking Arianna. They are wonderful together. Come we have work to do."

Lady Catherine is the head of the victualling staff. She asked Lady Arianna to assist her and her staff to prepare Arthur's travel provisions. Arianna was taught how to pack the dry meats in the dried deerhides and the grains were packed in what looked like burlap. This was done to keep the food dry and preserve it for the days to come. Water would be found near the campsights.

"Arianna, we pack so much because the men get so hungry when they travel, I think they are worse than a pack of wolves." Both women and staff laughed.

"Oh Sara, let us not forget the wine jugs. Arthur never travels without his wine."

Galahad made his usual notice me entrance.

"I dare say Galahad, your boots make more noise than those two swords out there."

"Alright Lady Catherine, I get the point." Galahad just stood there.

"Young man."

"Yes Lady Arianna."

"You can either help with the provisions or go and read your lessons for today. Then report to me on what they were about."

"My Lady, you are beginning to sound like a real mother."

"Mind your manners young man. Arianna has two children, she is a real mother."

Galahad chose to help instead of read.

"If I did not know any better, I would think my son was here. He does not like reading either."

As Galahad put the sack down he noticed Excalibur on the table. Without asking permission he grabbed her and ran into the courtyard.

"Galahad, where are you going?"

Before Arianna could catch up, Galahad was already in the courtyard, and very ready to play with the "BIG BOYS". As Galahad jumped over the wall with Excalibur raised, he rushed to Arthur and Gawain. Arthur's peripheral distraction caused a wound to his forearm. Arthur, being very angry, reaped at Galahad's Excalibur. As metal and metal met in anger, the sound was that of death.

"Have you gone mad boy? One of us could have been dead right now, all because you need to prove you are a man!"

Arthur looked at his wounded arm. There was a good amount of blood. Gawain came to Arthur's aid and wrapped his arm.

"I am so sorry My Lord."

"It is not your fault my friend, it is this boy's. Galahad do you realize I have enough problems with one son? I need not more with the other."

"ARIANNA!"—Catherine and Arianna came forward, while Galahad stood there completely embarrassed.

"Why is he here? Why is he not working with you?"

"I am sorry Sire. He grabbed the sword and ran. There was no stopping him."

Catherine tended Arthur's wound while Arianna retrieved Excalibur from the ground. The handle was like ice. "How could this be?" Arianna thought, the warm sun was shining on her. Excalibur was foretelling her own future. This she now knew.

Gawain handed Arthur his sword. As Arthur hung his Excalibur in her sheath he looked again at Arianna. The cold stare froze both of them.

Arthur suddenly felt bewitched. Was Arianna the Angel from Heaven or from Hell? Only God would know, and Arthur needed answers.

Chapter Twelve

MODRED

Modred lives in a beautiful sea side cottage. Arthur built this cottage for Guenevere and he after they were married. It stands on a hill over the ocean. From Modred's private quarters one could hear the waves crashing on the cliff.

"My Prince, Giles brings news. Arthur has ordered the dead buried and the village, whatever is left, burned to the ground."

"So, Arthur takes responsibility for his actions."

"My Prince, Arthur had nothing to do with Southampton."

Modred in anger slashed Henry's right forearm. Henry was shocked, holding the offensive gash.

"My Prince, Arthur..."

"QUIET!!" Modred strikes his face.

"My father is responsible for everything. Do you hear me!"

"Yes my Prince."

While Henry tended his wounds, Modred summoned Giles and Terrance to his woeful presence. Modred resembles Arthur-strong chin and body with long brown hair and brown eyes. Modred's ways have sculptured his features to look hard and cruel, where Arthur's face is commanding yet kind.

"Do you both think I am responsible?"

In unison, "No My Prince."

Yet they were both present at Modred's treachery. They carried out Modred's orders. They could still see the slaughter and smell the burning as if it were going on right now. All of Modred's followers were terrified of this madman. They were afraid if they walked away and gave Arthur back the allegiance they once had with this good king they would suffer the same fate.

Modred paced the floor. This room, of beautiful stained glass and gold stone walls was hardly a place for this brutal madman. Modred pounded his fist on the table.

"WHERE IS QUEEN MAB?"

Most of this madman's followers were once under Arthur's protection. Modred and his empty promises swayed them to himself. When they tried to retaliate, Modred's threats were too terrifying to deal with. These men have families to worry about. They knew Modred's highly paid guards would weed them out and their family and friends and their lands would be destroyed. They were very much afraid of Modred's friend The Evil Pagan, Queen Mab. Some had seen her, some had only heard about her. Some said she was beautiful, others said she was as ugly as her Black Magic. Nevertheless, Modred loved her and therefore there was no mercy or a way out. Modred wanted Arthur's throne and would stop at nothing to get it. Mab was in his heart and mind. Mab could not control her only son, Merlin. Merlin wanted nothing to do with Black Magic. Merlin only saw good for his powers. Arthur could not be touched either. He and Merlin were too close. Mab could not break them. She found her way through Modred and therefore used his greedy heart as her pawn.

"My Prince."
"Yes Giles."
"What would you have us do?"
"Send Harry and tell the men to prepare." He drew his sword and raised it.
"Prepare for the City of Northern Lights."
"The City of Northern Lights? Why there?"
Modred swung his sword. It gave the sound of the wind whipping through the walls.

"It is there my father will find his fate."

Chapter Thirteen

THE LADY OF THE LAKE

As the endless day continued, Arthur became more and more restless. Late noon had finally shown its face. In tradition, as usual, a feast was being prepared in the main square of Camelot. It did not matter if it were a celebration or an evening before battle, Arthur gathered his people to be together.

As Arthur and Merlin are walking through the square, they are both sampling the food.

"Merlin, I am confused. This woman Arianna, who is she?"

"Why do you ask?"

"I have trusted your better judgement for years, but this time I do not know."

"Sire?"

"Is she an omen a sign from Heaven or a sign from Hell?"

Merlin pulls his cloak over his shoulder as though hiding from Arthur.

"Why two Excalibur's? I only drew one from the stone. Yet they are exactly alike. Where did the other one come from?"

"How is your arm? Can you handle riding right now?" Arthur wore a puzzled look on his face. Arthur answered.

"I can ride. I will be alright Merlin."

"Then get into your riding attire."

Merlin then proceeded to the stables. Peter, a stable boy, was busy brushing Sir Julius, Arthur's horse.

"Young Peter, you care for these horses as though they are your children."

Peter smiled with so much pride.

"I love them Merlin. They are my friends."

"Well then, could you please saddle up Bennett, Julius and Brach for me?"

Peter stopped brushing the horses.

"They will be ready shortly."

"Thank you, Peter."

Merlin then proceeded to the galley.

"Lady Catherine, could you please spare Arianna for a little while?"

"Why?"

"His Lordship would like a conference with her." Arianna started to clean up. She thought to herself, "why would His Majesty wish to see me?"

"My Lady, meet us in the Round Table Room."

"I will be back shortly Catherine."

Arianna was not prepared for what she was in for. The guard opened the door and there stood King Arthur and Merlin in full riding attire. Arianna froze in her steps.

"My Lord, you sent for me?"

"You are a strange woman, I cannot help wondering." Merlin rudely stepped in front of them.

"Do you have Excalibur?"

"Right here."

"We are gong for a ride." Arianna was surprised.

"I do not understand."

"Arthur needs to speak with you privately."

Arianna did not have to feel for Excalibur under her apron. The sword's icy chill went through her dress and up her spine.

As they left the castle, Arianna felt her stomach grow tighter. She thought to herself "How do I tell him who I am? He will think I am some sought of crazy lady. It is bad enough I cannot explain it to myself, let alone King Arthur. Let alone Jack, if I ever see him or my children again."

They walked down to the gates where Arianna had arrived one day ago. Peter was standing there with all horses ready. Arthur helped Arianna to her saddle. He looked so inquisitive. Merlin and Arthur mounted their horses.

"Where do we go?"

"The City of Northern Lights."

"Sire?"

Arianna reached for Merlin's brown riding cloak. Merlin assured Arianna it was alright. According to all Arianna's books this was Arthur's last stop in life.

The afternoon was beautiful. The air crisp and cool as a mild breeze rustled through the trees. A sky of blue, with clouds of white just enough to decorate, enhanced by a bright warm sky. Arianna was riding between these two men, one a King, one a Master Warlock. Two great legends and she alone had the privilege of their company.

The city was two miles away from Camelot. The city was so breathtaking. How could one fathom that a war could be fought here? A King would die here!

The silence between the three was horrifically deafening. Every breath the horses made could be heard. Could Merlin and Arianna explain themselves? Arianna could not change history, but her very presence was already wreaking havoc. The question is, how and where?

The city was now in sight. Presently the three came through the vast trees. Hence the vision was of water, cool blue water. The sky kissed it blue and gave it radiant color. One problem: Arianna could swear this was Merlin's Pond. "I was just here a day ago or was I?"

Time was losing itself to disparity. Arthur dismounted first. He looked around. There were bittersweet memories on his face. He and Merlin helped Arianna off her horse. Arthur then placed Excalibur on the grass and instructed Arianna to do the same.

"Extraordinary, they are exactly alike. The only difference is on yours, Arianna, the crown over the dragon's head has worn a little."

"Sire, I am sorry about Galahad's behavior. Is your arm alright?" Arthur rubbed the wound.

"Galahad is an impetuous young man. He will come to his own someday. He has a big heart much like Arthur's. He shows much promise in becoming a good leader in the future."

"The birds make sweet music this day."

"They do, Arianna. They remind me of times past. When Guenevere and I would come to this place only to see the beauty in each other."

"My Lord Arthur, My Lady Arianna, come, the day will end and questions will have no answers."

"You are right Merlin," Arianna whispered.

"Merlin, how can I explain myself? Does The Lady of the Lake live here?"

Suddenly, with great fear in his voice, Arthur asked Arianna, "ARE YOU AN ANGEL FROM HELL OR FROM HEAVEN?"

Arthur's face grew pale, Arianna knew by his skin color her self-defense would not be an easy one. She felt herself ready to run away.

"I assure you Sire, I am only human." Arianna took a deep breath.

"My Lord Arthur, I am from a time you have not yet dreamed of. I cannot even begin to explain why I am here. All I can tell you is Merlin needed me and maybe somehow I needed Merlin and maybe even you too, My Lord."

Arthur, seeming somewhat enlightened, moves to lean his weary body on a tree. He folds his arms and with sarcasm he says, "All right, Merlin."

Arianna, sensing Arthur's dismayed response walks to the edge of the lake, turns, holding her body stiff, placing her hands tight behind her back.

"Please Sire, my name is Arianna Lawrence. I come from the year 1998."

"1998? MERLIN, WHAT GAMES DO YOU PLAY?"

"Sire please, hear Lady Arianna." Arianna now fears Arthur's authority.

"I was on holiday to London with my family."

"Your family?"

"Yes, I am married."

"I so gathered that by your ring."

"My husband is Jack Lawrence. I have two children-Alexis, age thirteen years and a son Joseph, age ten years."

Arthur, standing there in total disbelief, justifiably defends "What manner of fool do you take me for, both of you? Merlin I grow angry." Merlin reaches for Arthur's shoulder. Arthur pushes Merlin's hand away.

"Have I ever given reason for you to doubt me?"

"I cannot say you have, but then again there has been occasion."

"ENOUGH." Arthur's face now ridged.

"Come Arianna, stand here."

Merlin points to the ground on which he stands.

"Arthur, now you stand here. Take each others hands."

Arthur is now appearing to be more and more annoyed.

"Look at Lady Arianna's face. Tell me My King, what do you see?" Arianna's hands were now shaking. She looked into Arthur's eyes and then bowed her head. Arthur lifted her face to his. Fear and disparity filled his hand.

"I—I see a face of gentleness."

"Go on." Merlin's voice encouraging both of them.

"Yet your eyes have much suffering behind them." Arthur's face now showed some kind of concern.

"My Lady, may I show Arthur your life?"

"How can you?"

"Look at the lake, both of you. Images of Arianna's life will be shown to you." Arianna and Arthur now joined together in some disbelief.

"But Merlin, you know you cannot show the past or change it. Your powers only give you visions of the future, premonitions maybe."

"Arthur, please understand. With Arianna I cannot change anything either, but she is the future. Therefore everything, every image to be revealed is the future."

"HOLD each other."

"MY LADY OF THE LAKE!! DO—YOU—HEAR—ME?"

The lake moved as though whales were spyhopping all around. Out from the water a woman of great beauty emerged. Having starlit blonde hair, her face was of porcelain. Her eyes, sea blue and her lips, rose pink. She adorned a blue and white dress made of sea waves with a garland of gold around her lithe waste and one fastening her hair. The Lady's voice, so gentle.

"Merlin, my nephew, what do you wish?"

"Help Arthur see who Arianna is. She has come to help me but Arthur is afraid." Arthur and Arianna were astounded by this vision.

"Arthur, fear not."

Merlin and The Lady took water in their hands and threw it, as if it were a tapestry. Each part of Arianna's life showed in front of them.

"Arianna, Arthur, do not let go."

Arthur held tight to Arianna. The visions were horrible, so many conflicts. One was Arianna's brothers' need for constant help and attention .She was always kept in the shadows. They finally became estranged. The next vision shocked Arthur. A young man she knew raped Arianna at twenty years of age.

"No, Please. I do not want to remember."

This vision sickened and scared Arthur. A sickly mother, then her sudden death. Her brother's death. One vision shown Arianna over a sick man.

"Is this…"

"Yes, my husband. He has been ill for a long time. Please I cannot live this again."

Arthur now sees Arianna's son Joseph. He sees a younger version of Modred. Right in front of him was the same conflicts, the constant heartbreaking animosity he lives with day after day. Was there any more for her to give?

"Hold on a little longer Arianna."

The Lady then showed Arianna's wedding day and her children as babies. At least these were her happy times. Arianna smiled when she saw her babies. Then finally, Arianna's illness.

"Please no more, I cannot bear it!"

The beautiful Lady waved her arm and all the visions vanished. Tears fell on Arthur and Arianna. Then The Lady and Merlin took both EXCALIBURS, placing their blades in the cool water. This tapestry revealed Arianna finding Excalibur. Then her trail in Arthur's court, and the very moment they were living now.

Arianna sobbed uncontrollably. She fell to the ground. Arthur beheld her so close, rocking her. The Lady of the Lake wrapped her arms around both of them. Her beautiful dress seemed as though a security blanket, a blanket from all the frailties life had brought them. Merlin was standing ever so close, as though a guardian angel.

"As you can see Arthur, your life and Arianna's have echoed each other's in different ways. This is why time has found to put your kindred souls together. You must help each other find peace. One to live in peace until her days sees their close. The other to find peace before the final battles take his soul."

"Merlin, I take my leave now. Keep them close for whatever time allows. Arianna remember this day always. Time will not forget you." The Lady faded into the Lake. Arthur held onto Arianna, they could not let go.

"I am so sorry for doubting you, and you Merlin. God has sent you to me. I know this now."

"Merlin, are my days to be numbered?"

"I fear so."

"Will Arianna be with me in battle?"

"Only in Spirit My Lord."

"I cannot follow you, Sire."

"Are you the keeper of Excalibur?"

"For now she is. After your death Arthur, Excalibur will find a new keeper." Dusk now shows its oppressive face.

"Come, we must return. My people will wonder if Modred had his vengeance." Arthur picked up Arianna's Excalibur.

"Here, she belongs to you." Then Merlin gave Arthur his Excalibur. The three mounted their horses. Arianna took one last look at the lake, one more time to take in its beauty. She knew Modred would ravage its beauty.

"Good-bye Lady of the Lake. Take care and be careful." She felt guilty not telling Arthur his life's course. The only comfort Arianna took was in knowing that in her time, beauty took its solace again, in this place of magic.

There was a mile of conversation in front of them.

"Lady Arianna."

"Sire."

"Please, I am Arthur."

For the moment Arianna could finally feel some peace of mind. She stopped her horse momentarily and thought "So be it." Arianna took a deep breath while saying "Arthur," and smiled.

"Please tell me, if it is not so painful. Who raped you?"

"A young man I courted."

"His name?"

"What does it matter?"

"His name please!" Arianna choked. Her King wished her to reveal this deep secret she had hidden away.

"His name is Gregory."

"A curse be on Gregory's head."

"If that were so Merlin. Arianna hung her head. The scar this crime left behind ran deep. Arthur again is trying to learn what happened to Arianna.

"Arianna, please tell us." Arianna took a deep breath.

"He wanted his way with me. I said "NO." We did not know each other long enough, nor did I love him. Relief, finally, revealing this secret she covered for so long. Angrily she tells her King.

"Arthur, he took me with malice. I hate him for feeling all these years that it was my fault." Arthur realized her secrecy.

"You did not tell any one?"

"No, not one soul until today. I was afraid. I covered my wounds and buried them deep. It seems as though I am always covering my wounds and burying them."

"I know my dear. They somehow manage to open and show themselves. There is no easy way. Your son Arianna, tell me about Joseph."

"My son Joseph is a younger version of yours. I have no peace with him, between his learning problems, his compulsive nervous habits and his constant opposition. I feel as though I am always in the battlefield. I love him so much yet he uses that love as a weapon against me. There are days when I question myself, blame myself for who he has become. Oh Arthur what will we do?"

"Believe me Arianna, when I say I feel the same as you. There are days when I wish that Modred was never born. There are days when I hate him as much as I love him."

"I too, about Joseph."

"Parents carry their crosses in different ways. It is how we carry them that is important."

"Merlin, you are wise."

"I agree Arianna." Merlin is feeling a little parental towards both of them.

"Thank you. Both of you."

"Arianna, may I hold your hand?"

Arianna placed her hand in Arthur's. They held on to each other all the way back to Camelot.

The window lamps lit up Camelot. Coming up the causeway they could see the torches lit in the Village Square. The Three riders could smell the feast being cooked. It was an inviting homecoming.

Chapter Fourteen

THE VILLAGE SQUARE

Out of the quiet came Galahad's voice from the gate watchtower.

"OPEN THE GATE. THEY ARE HERE!!"

Through the thunder of chains Arthur could hear Galahad running down the stairs.

"Uncle Arthur, thank God you are alive."

The crowd roared with happiness. Merlin assured everyone they were safe the whole time. Arthur's Knights Sir Gawain, Sir William, Sir Frederick and Sir Percy formed an Honor Guard around King Arthur. King Arthur extended his hand to invite Arianna and Merlin in the circle. The three were then escorted to the main table in front of the castle steps.

Un-be-knowst to them, Modred and his guards were outside the city walls listening, waiting for their time in battle.

"My father finds the love of a woman again. Does he not remember my mother? He thinks bedding this woman will erase her memory. Two days hence he will remember her. I will use the sword of the Lady Morgana. Mab will give it power to end his days. This I pledge this night."

"Why not take him here?"

"No Giles. I want The Lady of the Lake to see my vengeance. I want her to see her sister Mab's power will always rule this place."

In the square the gaiety at least for this evening continued. Once Arthur, Merlin and Arianna were near the steps, Peter the stable boy escorted the horses back.

"Peter."

"My Lord."

"Please get Her Ladyship a proper scabbard for Excalibur." Peter smiled.

"Right away Sire."

"My Lord."

"What is it Gawain?"

"Your men seek counsel with you."

"I assure you I am alright."

"We can see that Sire, but there are other matters to discuss." Arthur took his leave, entering the castle in protest. Each man stood by his chair in the Round Table Room. Arthur placed Excalibur in her rightful spot.

"Gentlemen, why are we here when the feast is outside?"

"Sire you look different. Are you bewitched?"

"BEWITCHED? Have you all gone mad?"

"Sire, we are very worried about this woman."

"William, Lady Arianna is a good and peaceful woman. She is probably the bravest woman I have ever met."

"Sire, word has traveled. She is married."

"Percy, I am quite aware she is married. She told me so herself."

"My Lord, are you sure?"

"Ralph, I am not, nor is she, an adulterer. Nothing has happened or will happen between us. So help me God. Now our families await us. Let us join them."

"Gawain, any word on Modred?"

"I am sorry My Lord, that is what we are afraid of. Sire your arm. How is the wound?" Arthur rubbed his forearm.

"It is fine, barely a scratch."

The crowd watched for Arthur's presence. Exiting the castle with his Knights, he was greeted cheerfully. "LONG LIVE KING ARTHUR—LONG LIVE KING ARTHUR" again and again they shouted. Arthur's heart was touched. He knew his people loved him.

Lady Catherine and Galahad were at the end of the table chatting. While Merlin sat at the bottom step doing magic tricks with the children, games were being played. There was a group of men playing tug of war. Children are racing each other. Stuffed cloths being tossed by other children, just like monkey in the middle. Arianna wished she could stay there, just freeze time. If it were only possible. Her heart knew at daybreak all would end. Arthur could not help but notice Arianna stood alone sipping a chalice of wine. He could not help but feel that being alone was commonplace for her.

"Arianna."

"Arthur, you startled me."

"I am sorry."

"I am enjoying watching the children."

"Why are you alone?"

"Am I? I really did not notice. I suppose when you have spent, as much time as I being alone, it becomes a natural part of you. When Jack was so sick, his illness and the children took so much of my time that having time and taking time to be alone became my best friend."

"Funny, I assumed so."

"What do you mean?"

Arthur dismissed the question with a kiss on Arianna's hand. "Come, sit next to me. I do not know about you but I could eat a horse."

They sat at the table and the dinner fanfare was given. Merlin sat next to Arianna.

"Merlin, have you performed some magic this night? The sky is magical, all the constellations have joined us."

"I wish I could take credit, but we know who the magician is."

Arthur stood. "A prayer please. Let us be thankful to God for this feast. For the Love and the strength of our families and our new friend. May God go with us and give us hope."

All answered "AMEN!!"

The feast lasted most of the evening. It was time for all of them to be a family. Arthur was so pleased with his people he said a silent prayer. He thanked God for his people and for Modred on this magical night.

Chapter Fifteen

DAYBREAK – DAWN TO DEATH

After not sleeping for nearly two days and consuming two chalices of wine Arianna soon fell into a deep sleep. The sleep though was not a restful one. It was more like a twilight sleep, in and out of dreaming. Her thoughts ran from what transpired with Arthur, to her fears about the forthcoming battle, to Jack, his illness and the hospitals. Arianna had a fight with Alexis before she left.

"Dear God, why was I so gruff with her? All Alexis wanted to do was go rollerblading with Kevin. There is nothing wrong with that." Arianna sat up in Guenevere's bed. She then stepped out on the verandah.

"Dear God Arianna, Alexis is thirteen. Can you remember being thirteen? She's not a little girl any longer. She's a straight "A" student, a responsible human being. I think I am doing a good job raising her. Don't act like your mother. Try and remember what it felt like. When I get home I promise myself I will start relaxing around her. I hope I get home."

Arianna fell back to sleep. At least for the most part a restful one, until Four A.M, when she heard Arthur and Galahad in the hall arguing. She ajared the door to listen.

"Uncle Arthur, please let me go with you. I am already a full-grown man. I can handle a sword and shield."

"Galahad."

"A bow and arrow---Please let me go!"

"Galahad you are barely a man. Your body may show that you are a man, but your mind and heart are not there yet."

"Uncle Arthur…"

"I already said I need you here."

"Uncle Arthur Please!"

"GALAHAD, NO!! Now you listen, I am about to lose one son. In fact I have already lost him. His wife, his mother has bewitched him. He was a good boy a long time ago. Now he is the puppet of three women, ALL WITCHES, however you wish to look at them."

"I HATE MY OWN SON! DO NOT LET ME LOSE THE ONE I LOVE. Keep Lady Arianna safe. When I return, she will have to return home."

Arianna came out of her room. "My Lady, good morning. I hope you slept well."

"I did Sire, to a point."

"Both of you keep each other close. Now Galahad help me into my armor. I leave at daybreak.

The morning meal was brought to Arthur's chamber. He feasted on bread, fruit and his favorite goats' milk. Galahad helped Arthur finish preparing, took one look at him in full dress armor and in haste hugged him. "I love you uncle Arthur." Then left.

At Arthur's urgent request Sir Gawain and Lady Catherine were summoned to his quarters. Arianna and the two greeted their good mornings, but Arianna chose to stay outside.

"Sire, you sent for us?"

"Please sit down." Arthur gestures for them to sit. Gawain chose to stand.

"Sire, let me go with you."

"My dear brother, I need you here. I need the brother I love the most to guard my home. His home."

Sir Gawain knelt down on one knee to kiss Arthur's ring, then said these words: "I will keep your castle safe my King." Catherine watched with such pride.

"I will take care of him Sire." Arthur then kissed Lady Catherine on both cheeks.

"Please, now leave me in peace."

Lady Catherine and Lady Arianna's eyes met. Words were not needed to be spoken. Their facial expressions were only of worry.

After the door closed Arthur knelt by his bed taking Excalibur to his chest.

"Lord take care of my men. Keep a close eye on them. Help my son see your ways. Keep my home safe for my people. Please Lord if not, Your Will Be Done." Arthur stood, put Excalibur in her sheath and took one last look at Camelot from his verandah. A peculiar chill ran through him.

"I AM SO AFRAID LORD. I AM SO AFRAID."

Daylight broke through the shutters. Arianna's heart raced. Dawns bells broke through the silence. One ring-two rings-three rings-four rings. On the fifth ring Arthur's men sounded revelry fan fare. The stable boys led by Peter brought the horses to the Village Square. King Arthur, his Knights and his armies were dressed in their finest of Armor. Arthur stood at the top step of the castle. Sir Ralph, Sir Gawain, Sir William, Sir Frederick, Sir Percy and finally Sir John joined him. Merlin, Catherine and Arianna stood at the bottom step.

"Arianna, do you have Excalibur with you?" Arianna moved her apron to the side.

"Look Merlin, Peter gave me this fine sheath for her." Merlin knew Excalibur was safe. Catherine looked confused.

Peter brought Arthur a chalice of wine. Arthur lifted the chalice.

"MEN OF CAMELOT I SALUTE YOU! MAY GOD GO WITH US!!"

He drank the wine down as though trying to chase away all the ghosts that haunted him.

Arthur's Knights and armies lifted their swords. As though in one voice they chanted "LONG LIVE KING ARTHUR. LONG LIVE KING ARTHUR. LONG LIVE KING ARTHUR!" Their voices roared through the hills of Camelot. Arthur tried to fight tears but Arianna and Catherine saw them. Arthur beckoned Merlin and Arianna before him.

"Merlin, wait two hours and follow me." Merlin saw the fear in his eyes. Then the vision of Arthur's death was placed before him. Merlin shuddered.

"I will follow you My Lord." Arianna touched Merlin's shoulder.

"You saw it, the vision."

"Henceforth Arianna, Excalibur will signal you. Wait for her signal then leave." Merlin left before Arthur mounted his horse.

"Arianna."

Arianna looked into Arthur's fearful eyes.

"My Lord. What do you wish?"

"I have a request for you." Arianna reaches to touch Arthur's forearm. The gauntlet feels cool from the cold morning breeze.

"Anything Sire." Arianna wished she could hold him there and never let go of him. Arthur knew by her touch and joined her hand with his.

"I wish a favor from you."

" A favor, what kind of favor?" Arianna blushed.

"My Lord, I understand." Arianna searched for what she could give Arthur. She then took off her cross. A gold cross bearing a heart with a diamond in the middle. Arianna placed it in Arthur's hand.

"Jack's parents gave it to me. I have always felt that it protected me. Take it."

"Arianna, please put it on for me." Arianna placed the cross on Arthur's neck. Arthur then kissed Arianna's hand and then with such gentleness placed a kiss on her cheek.

"Thank you. Take care of Galahad."

"I will Arthur." Arthur smiled. Arianna called him by his given name. Arianna knew he needed to here it.

"I know he is angry with me. That is why he is not here. Please tell him I love him."

"I will Arthur."

Arthur mounted his horse, as did all his men to follow him. The fan fare followed. The gates opened and Arthur led his Knights and two hundred men out of the Village Square.

The sight was glorious to behold. Arianna's heart sank in her chest. She knew the next time she saw Arthur would be in death.

Chapter Sixteen

GALAHAD'S PROMISE

Arianna stood by the castle steps. The sun was starting to shine. The sky never looked more beautiful than this one morning.

"Lady Arianna."

"Galahad, where have you been?" Galahad is standing by the door checking to see if the area is clear.

"I could not say good-bye."

"Your uncle needed you, he needed all the love and support you could have given him."

"He said he loves me." Arianna beckons Galahad to join her on the steps.

"Galahad, your uncle loves you more than you know. Arthur would have a sword impale his heart before it would impale yours. He is a rare man."

"I know he has more reason to hate me than Modred."

"Why is that?"

"My father was his most precious Knight. His name was Lancelot. While Uncle Arthur was away fighting wars to keep us free, while he fought the Romans over the HOLY GRAIL and the rights of true Christian people, my father and his beautiful wife Queen Guenevere had an affair. Uncle Arthur could have had them killed, but he chose to banish them. When my mother heard of the news she became so ill she died."

"So what does that have to do with hating you?"

"My father hurt Uncle Arthur, he could have hated me for being his son. Instead when he heard I was a boy without a home he brought me here. He in turn became my father." Galahad lets out a shy kind of laugh.

"God knows I had enough mothers too, between Lady Catherine and the others." Arianna put her arm around Galahad's shoulders.

"So, is this so terrible?"

"No, he gave me everything I needed, even he took my fathers sin from me. His Majesty gave me so much love. It is amazing how much love he has to give everyone. I wish we all had this amount of love to give in return."

"Fathers and mothers are like that Galahad. They give more than they receive."

Galahad sat on that bottom step staring at the gate.

"Ahhh, I know what your problem is."

"What is that?"

"Arthur gave you so much that you feel you must fight for him. Perhaps give your life for him?" Galahad's expression was that of deducement yet surprised.

"How did you know?"

"Arthur has given you so much, that you have made yourself feel guilty for his love. Do not. Galahad you are a young man. You have a long life ahead of you." Galahad realizes Arianna is helping him understand why Arthur loves him so much.

"Galahad, someday in your future there will be a time when you can honor King Arthur. Let that time come in its time. Do not push the moments now. Seize the day, then your heart will guide you." Galahad stood then and poured two chalices of water.

"Tell me about your son Joseph."

Arianna closes her eyes going deep within herself, asking herself how do I explain Joseph's A.D.H.D. and Tourette's? Opening her eyes, she takes a deep breath.

"Joseph is a good boy. He has some physical and learning problems."

"Learning problems? What do you mean?"

"Joseph's brain is kind of scrambled up. His body and brain chemistry are not quite normal." Galahad, being an astute young man, reacts to Joseph's problem.

"You mean, as if he were drunk?"

"Yes, you could say that."

"So what problems does this bring?"

"It disables him to take on responsibilities. To do the simplest task is sometimes too hard. He has problems understanding words, taking directions. In all, understanding his world is one big pool of frustration and sometimes, alienation."

"My Lady, you mean like having Queen Mab in his head?" Arianna smirks.

"That is a good assessment Galahad, I would have never thought of it that way." Galahad takes Arianna's hand, comforting her.

"This disability has made life hard for all of us. I told Uncle Arthur that somedays I hate him." She drops her head in shame.

"I do not hate him, I love him with all my heart. HE IS MY SON!"

"This was hard for you to say."

"Galahad, I wish I could fight the monsters for him, but I cannot. He has to learn to fight them. We have to fight them together and win the battle. I do not want my son to grow up and become like Modred. But sometimes I admit the battles get too hard for this mother to bare."

With these words they saw Merlin leave to follow Arthur. Galahad again takes Arianna's hand.

"Can I help you fight these battles with him?"

"Oh Galahad, I wish you could. You could be a big brother to him, but alas my home is too far away."

"Then give this to Joseph." Galahad placed his dagger in Arianna's hand.

"Tell him this will fight the battles."

"I cannot take this."

"Please, I insist." Galahad closed Arianna's hand around the gold dagger.

"Lady Arianna, I promise you that I will try to mature first and learn well." Arianna hugged Galahad like a mother to a son.

"I am proud of you." Galahad felt Excalibur's hilt on his leg.

"My Lady, could I hold Excalibur?"

"I guess for just a moment." Galahad took Excalibur from her guardian's hands then took Excalibur to his breast and said these words: "I wish to become like Uncle Arthur and make him proud. Someday when I have a son, I will carry Uncle Arthur and your example with me to raise him, well sturdy and steadfast. With all the love in my heart."

Then, just as a boy, he played with Excalibur as though he were a Knight.
"Look My Lady," and he bowed as if a true Knight.
"Someday I will be a Knight." They laughed.
"Yes you will. Yes you will Sir Galahad!"
Then "Sir Galahad" gently gave Excalibur to the Lady Arianna.

Chapter Seventeen

QUEEN MAB

"M-E-R-L-I-N." The sound broke Merlin's peaceful solitary ride.

"M-E-R-L-I-N." Merlin stopped dead in his tracks. He then looked around. The forest was clear of humans. Except for a family of deer one hundred feet in front of him and some crows, the area was peaceful. The wind rustled the trees a little louder. Sir Bennett, Merlin's horse, twitched his ears while tightening his neck. It was Bennett's way of showing caution, and Merlin heedfully listened.

Merlin shouted "IS ANYBODY THERE!?" while kicking Bennett to move, but he would not.

Again "M-E-R-L-I-N." This time Merlin drew forth his sword. Sir Bennett started prancing nervously.

"Whomever you are, show yourself."

"M-E-R-L-I-N—N-N-N." The sound echoed through the trees. Merlin took hold of his senses.

"There is only one person in this world who could frighten me like this. MAB!! COME FORWARD!!"

"M-E-R-L-I-N-N-N-N." Merlin tightened his grip on Bennett's bridal and his sword.

"SHOW YOURSELF MAB!! I HAVE NO TIME FOR YOUR VICIOUS GAMES!!"

"You call this vicious? I call it having a good time." Mab's sultry raspy voice came from behind a tree.

"MAB, ENOUGH! COME OUT MAB!!"

Mab finally showed herself. For an evil woman, she was beautiful. Mab stood five feet six inches tall, having a lithe figure, beautiful long black hair with red highlights in the sunlight. An olive complexion and the face of a goddess with glorious ebony eyes. A magnificent specimen of a woman WITH A HEART OF STONE!

"You never change Mab."

"I am your mother. For once can you not call me Mother?' Being totally evasive of the question.

"I see we are in our red mood."

"Oh, you noticed. I am beautiful in it, am I not?" As a little girl would, she waved her skirt around.

"What fairy paid the price for that dress?" Merlin held fast on his sword.

"Oh Merlin." Mab waved her arm and every animal screamed in pain.

"MAB, STOP NOW!!" She waved her arm and again the screams got louder.

"MAB STOP!!" Merlin jumped off Sir Bennett throwing his sword toward Mab just short of killing her.

"MOTHER STOP!! NOW, DAMN IT, NOW!!"

In a flinch, the screams stopped.

"What is it you want Mother?"

"My son, I love when your blue eyes get that fiery angry look. My son, my dear son." Mab stroked Merlin's face.

"Your plan with this Arianna will not work." Merlin's face now wracked with worry.

"Keep away from her Mab."

"Oh, I cannot touch her. My magic cannot touch her." Merlin's body now in a cold sweat.

"What? What do you mean?" Mab knows she is getting to Merlin.

"Arianna is not from our time, her substance here is only YOUR ILLUSION! To help YOU ESCAPE YOUR MISTAKE!!" With every word the sky thundered.

"Now give mother a kiss." Merlin put his hands over his face.

"AHH. YOUR KISSES ARE POISON!! They poison hearts and souls. You steal lives Mab, not honor them. You take peoples' minds Mab. You put them into your slavery." Merlin is trying to hold on to his sanity.

"YOU DESTROY THEM WITH DEBAUCHERY!!"

Mab draws Merlin's sword from the tree it landed in. Holding it high, her sultry voice sounded deeper in anger.

"YOU WILL FAIL, YOUR SWORD WILL FAIL! Arianna will never be able to foil your sin. Arthur, you and Arianna will all founder at Modred's hand. TODAY, I PROMISE YOU!!" In a frightening heartbeat she vanished. Merlin's sword hit the ground with a heart-stopping clang.

Merlin stood in shock. All his life he tried not to let Mab intimidate him. Today she succeeded. He knelt down to pick up his sword, frightening chills now entering his body. Dejection ravaged him. Merlin stayed on both knees, his heart pounding sweat pouring down on his pale face. In one hard breath he screamed "A-R-I-A-N-N-A!!"

Sir Bennett felt his pain. This faithful steed tried to comfort his master by caressing his snout on Merlin's shoulder. Merlin sat back on his heels. In total confusion he kept repeating "I must get to Arthur, I must get to Arthur."

In the safe confines of the castle, Arianna and Galahad were now entering the Drawing Room. A sudden gust of wind opened the shutters. "A-R-I-A-N-N-A" the wind screamed. Arianna and Galahad looked strangely at each other.

"Galahad, did you hear that?" Arianna's arms prickled with goose bumps. Galahad was so confused.

"What was that?" Arianna ran to the window searching for Merlin, then frantically ran out the door. Merlin was nowhere in sight.

TIME WAS NOW OF AN ESSENCE.

Chapter Eighteen

EMPIRE ROOM-DALTON

"Joseph come on! Mom should be back soon and then we will go for dinner."

"Daddy, after dinner can I come back down and watch some movies with the other kids?"

"What about me Dad, can I go with her."

"No brat, I want to do something on my own."

"Enough name calling Alexis."

"But Dad I've been with him all day. I want to be with other kids my own age." Joseph threw his toy on the ground.

"Huh, but that's not fair. I can't be with anyone my own age." Both children looked as though they were in a boxing match. Jack looked as if he was ready to call the British police.

"That is enough, both of you! When your mother gets back we will decide what we are doing."

"Please Dad, can I have time with the other kids? Carol and Kevin are leaving in two days. I'd like some time with them." Jack's neck is tensing up. He is holding on to his shoulder.

"OK, OK."

"Hey what about me?"

"Joseph, when you're older I'll let you do some of these things too." Joseph is now stamping his feet, making Jack very embarrassed.

"Dad it's not fair!"

"Mr. Lawrence maybe I can help you."

"I don't think anyone can help. Kids. I think I need a break."

"Well then I think I have the answer."

"What's that Martin?"

"After Mrs. Lawrence and you have your dinner, both of you can enjoy a drink in the lounge and Alexis could be with her friends. As for Joseph, he can go to the pool for a splash party and ice cream." Jack sat back with some relief on his anxiety-ridden face.

"Think of it. You and your wife can have some time alone and the children will be off doing whatever with the supervision they need."

Martin poured Jack a mug of ale.

"By the way, where is your lovely wife?"

"She is off on a horseback riding expedition. Arianna said she would be back by five o'clock. Seems as though she's a little late."

"Where did she go?"

"Warwick Riding Academy in Westminster."

"Oh, it is lovely there. A husband and wife run it. Yes, that is it. You see, the horses are named after famous Knights. It is an extraordinary place. The scenery is quite beautiful."

"Is it really?"

"Mostly soul searching. The tour is the ruins of Camelot and Merlin's Pond."

"Merlin's Pond?"

"It is the lake where Merlin threw Excalibur after King Arthur's death. It is all very mythical."

Jack folds his arms and with dismay says "sounds like I missed a great day."

"Another mug of ale?"

"Please."

"More like an unusual day. It is the type of journey you take if you have a love for history."

"Well, that's Arianna. She'll read or watch anything historical. It would be of no surprise to me if she jumped into one of her books."

Martin now in complete wonderment thinks to himself "I wonder if she is the one."

"You know Mr. Lawrence, Mrs. Lawrence is to be admired."

"Admired?"

"It is a rare quality in a woman."

"What is that?"

"Loving history, especially male dominant history."

"Martin, she is really running late. It's six o'clock."

"I would not worry Mr. Lawrence, maybe the tour ran late."

"Mr. Lawrence, do you play chess?" Jack was like a schoolboy eager to start the game.

"Indeed I do."

"Care to join me in a game? The hotel has a beautiful chess set. Unfortunately it does not get used very often."

"Sounds like a plan."

Martin and Jack went to the lounge to set up the chess set.

"Martin?"

"Yes sir."

"I think since Ari is running late I will take the kids for an early dinner. If Ari calls please let me know."

"What about the game?"

"Oh, we will definitely play later, if Arianna does not get back."

"Very good sir."

Chapter Nineteen

PETER-THE STABLE BOY

Arianna knew it was time to prepare for her journey back. She had no idea how long-a day, a week. All she knew was the inevitable.

"Lady Arianna, can I help you?"

"Please Peter, I would like to see Sir Brach."

"Pardon me for saying this, but it is unusual for a lady to be in my stables."

"I know Peter, I just want to make sure my horse and saddlebag are ready for traveling."

"Where are you going My Lady?"

"Sooner or later I must go home."

"Home?"

"Oh no My Lady, please stay."

"Why Peter?"

"You bring a smile to His Majesty's face." All during their conversation Peter is preparing the feed bags for Brach and for Sir Gawain's horse, also Galahad, and Peter's own horse, Beth.

"How do you know all this?"

"All the servants noticed. King Arthur has been happy since you came. The provision maid said he is eating well. My Lord even finished his wine yesterday. My Lady, His Lordship is such a kind man, but he is a lonely man. He needs someone like you to stay with him and help him."

"Peter, do you realize I am married? My family needs me also."

"I am aware of your marriage My Lady, but King Arthur needs you. You see, I wish to see my King happy." Arianna is beginning to feel a little guilty by now but she must go.

"I know you do and so do I. I will tell you what I can do." Arianna walked over to Sir Brach and while he ate she brushed him tenderly. The snort he gave told Arianna he appreciated the attention.

"You are good with horses My Lady."

" I love animals." Peter was patiently waiting for an answer.

"Now, how could you help King Arthur?"

"In a few months before the cold returns, I will return. I know it is not what you wish to hear, but I am married and I must return to my husband. Now, where is my saddle and saddlebag?" Peter brought her to where the horses armor was stored. The area was empty except for four saddles and one saddlebag, hanging over a wooden bar. It was an eerie emptiness. She checked her belongings and everything was in order. Her camcorder and camera were still there. If only I could film this. But she could not take the chance. How could she explain modern technology?

"Peter?"

"Sir Gawain, may I help you?"

"Lady Arianna, what are you doing in here?"

"Peter was so kind as to help me check on my horse."

"Oh, I see. Peter is my horse ready?"
"Of course sir. He has eaten and has been brushed."
"Good Lad."
"Thank you sir."
"Very good. Make them ready. We have some practicing to do."
"Sir Gawain, what do you mean by practicing?"
"I will explain."
"All right Sir Gawain."
"If Galahad wishes to become a Knight then he must attend to his lessons." Arianna handed Galahad's bridal to Peter.
"May I watch?" Gawain gave a kind of clearing of the throat noise.
"I do not think so Lady Arianna! It is mostly the kind of thing us men do alone."
"I see."
"Do you take lessons too Peter?"
"Oh yes My Lady, Sir Gawain is training me also." Sir Gawain picked up his whip and hit the fence with it. Arianna knew plainly that this was the signal to leave. Arianna put her finger to her chin and pouted her lips.
"I think I will see what Catherine is up to." As she was leaving Galahad walked in.
"My, my young man. YOU look most handsome in your armor." Galahad smiled from ear to ear.
"Thank you Lady Arianna."
While walking out, Arianna looked back only to see Peter being fitted into his armor. One thing ran through her mind: " It is a shame all boys have to grow up."

Chapter Twenty

ARIANNA'S CONFESSION

On the way back to the castle Arianna stood alone in the Village Square. She took Excalibur out from behind her apron, then proceeded to draw her from her sheath. "Please Excalibur, give me a sign. Merlin said you would. The suspense is hurting my heart. Can I face the inevitable?"

For the first time she paid attention to her reflection in the swords blade. Her long brown hair was now in beautiful braids. The dress was for a woman of royalty. It was the color of salmon with beige and white satin about the collar and sleeves. There was one thing missing.

"Dear God, look at me. I look like royalty but I do not feel like it. I am just plain Arianna from Queens, New York. Yet here I am in King Arthur's courtyard waiting to help Merlin. How could this have happened?"

Exhaustion finally caught up. Arianna found herself staring at Excalibur, her mind wandering.

"Oh Excalibur, what am I doing here? I have a family, a family that needs me. I don't belong here. I cannot explain to myself how I got here. I wish I could change things but I cannot. Funny, I cannot even change the way things are at home either, no matter how much I try. Sometimes I feel like a beautiful ship I once read about. She sailed on a beautiful voyage only to find obstacles in her way. She never completed her journey. She foundered. I AM TIRED. No matter how much I try to help my family, I do not think they really need me. I do not think they hear my good sense or that I am good enough. Oh, I am good enough as long as I take care of them. There are times when I feel my husbands' illness gives him license to dictate how we live. There is no partnership. He tells me to take care of yourself. How can I? I am just a piece of debris. Like the ship that sank." The tears came running.

"There are too many people missing in my life, Excalibur. Too many people I love. My mother, my brother, good and faithful friends all dead and now I am about to see Arthur die and leave Merlin. How can I bear it, that when I return home what will I do without Merlin? He has given me more friendship than any friend has or brother could give. I love Merlin. I love Arthur very much." From feeling morose came a crazy kind of laugh.

"You know Excalibur, maybe suicide could be an option."
Out of the silence came Lady Catherine's voice.
"Arianna, what are you doing?" Arianna hurried to compose herself.
"What are you doing here by yourself." Catherine looked at Arianna's tearful face.

"Are you alright my dear?" Catherine gave her a cloth so Arianna could wipe the tears away. Through sounds of sobbing Arianna tries explaining herself.

"Actually, I was wondering how Merlin and His Majesty are? I am so worried."

"I know my dear, we all are." Both women hold hands with a far away expression on their faces.

"I am just glad that Gawain was chosen to stay home. Do you think me selfish?"

"Not at all Catherine. We all wish to protect our children and husbands from harm."

"I wish I could see those gates open with Arthur and all of them returning home."

" I wish the same Catherine, I wish the same."

"Now, speaking of harm, please put that sword away. Preferably in a closet." Arianna felt she and Excalibur were threatened.

"I cannot, I cannot." Her voice sobbing from the request made by Catherine.

"Arianna, you do not have to get so upset about a little request."

"You do not understand. His Majesty and Merlin told me to keep Excalibur with me at all times."

Catherine looks at Arianna befuddled by such a strange request. She then asks, "Why?"

"I know that all I can tell you is those are my orders." Catherine now understands Arianna's cause. At least she thinks she does.

"Well then, they will be respected."

"Thank you."

"Please, no disrespect intended. Please put Excalibur in her sheath."

No sooner did Arianna put Excalibur in her scabbard a strange icy chill went up her spine. Modred was near Arthur. Soon she would have to leave. Can she find the strength?

"Arianna, come lets watch the boys practice."

The ladies walked through the stables and into the archery court. Peter stood practicing with the javelin. As the ladies stood by the protective brick wall Peter caught sight of them. He stood tall, took the stance and shot-put the javelin, hitting its mark one hundred and fifty feet right smack in the black mark Gawain painted between two crossed beams. The ladies applauded.

"Now Young Peter, if you could foil as well as you shot-put, we would not have a problem."

"That is quite alright Peter, your father will be proud of you anyway." Peter was standing quite proud.

"Thank you Lady Catherine."

"Who is his father?"

"Why, Sir William my dear. I thought you knew."

"I did not Catherine." Arianna felt a little foolish not knowing who Peter's father is.

"Now it is Galahad's turn." Gawain stepped over to where Galahad waited. He helped Galahad secure his breast plate and shoulder piece.

"We do not wish any harm done young man. Galahad, secure your gauntlets."

"Yes sir, I will."

"Are you ready young man?"

"Not yet Sir. I would like to ask Lady Arianna a favor."

"A favor?" Arianna looked very curious.

"What kind of favor?"

Galahad took his helmet off, walked over to the ladies, and now Catherine is very curious.

"I wonder what he wants."

He stood in front of Lady Arianna kneeling down on one knee.

"Oh, what is this?"

He then took her right hand and kissed it.

"Lady Arianna could I please use Excalibur to practice my swordplay exercise?"

"I do not know, Galahad." All the while holding onto her hilt tight.

"Go on Arianna, I do not think His Majesty would mind." Even Peter ran over to the rescue.

"Oh, please My Lady." Arianna smiled at Peter's boyish request. She then untied her apron and brought forth-beautiful Excalibur. Galahad was so pleased he kissed Arianna on the cheek, then felt very embarrassed.

"Oh Thank you!"

Gawain commented "I cannot believe there are two of them. Let us see what she's got, and you too my good lad," patting Galahad on the back. Galahad and Sir Gawain walked to the practice area.

"Galahad."

"Yes sir."

"Put the sword in your sheath." Galahad obeyed.

Gawain walked about ten feet away, fastened his helmet and fixed his eyes on Galahad.

"NOW GALAHAD, DRAW!"

Whence Galahad drew Excalibur, she made the sound of a bell. Taken back, Gawain and Galahad paused feeling eerie.

Then Gawain commanded: "Galahad, lunge and swing!"

Galahad obeyed the exercise.

Gawain then commanded: " Reap—reap" as he did the same, moving forward.

"Swing high Galahad. Swing high. LUNGE AT ME." Galahad moved quickly obeying every command. Whence the two swords clashed the sound of heaven overtook them. With every lunge, every clash, every reap, the swords music was beautiful.

Sir Gawain commanded: "STOP!"

"This is truly the sword of a good king." He then knelt before Excalibur. Galahad stood frozen, completely amazed and knelt himself. Peter jumped over the wall running over to Galahad.

"She is truly a beautiful sword."

Arianna and Catherine joined them. Galahad then kissed Excalibur, returning her to her guardian.

Galahad's noble gesture made Arianna wish Joseph was there to take example of these two fine young men.

"My God, no wonder why His Lordship wishes her with you at all times. You are her keeper, her defender." Arianna's eyes wandered into the forest, she became vague. Her thoughts went on Merlin.

"I wonder if he is all right, I am so worried for him.

The exercise ended.

Chapter Twenty-One

WAR GAMES

"Mr. Lawrence is getting worried Dorothy."

"I know, Martin."

"It seems as though I hope Edmund finally found the guardian for Excalibur. He is taking much too long." Martin looked at his watch. It was already seven-thirty.

"If they do not return by the light of the North Star, history might be changed."

"Dorothy, we will say our prayers."

"Keep Mr. Lawrence occupied."

"He took the children to have their dinner. I have arranged for them to have some activity this evening."

"Oh dear, I hope Mr. Lawrence takes on my suggestion to play chess. He is most anxious that Mrs. Lawrence has not yet returned."

"He is a good man and a good father. I can see it in his eyes when he speaks about Mrs. Lawrence."

" I get this feeling that for some odd reason he does not know how to express it. I know this because it took Edmund a long time to break out of his shell. I hope it does not take Mr. Lawrence that long. He does not realize Mrs. Lawrence needs the reassurance. He does not see how much she is falling apart."

Both hear footsteps coming in the direction of the office.

"Martin, I'm glad you are still here. I'm sorry, I did not realize you had company."

"Mr. Lawrence, this is Dorothy Winters. She runs the Warwick Riding Academy."

"Is Arianna alright?"

"Oh yes, perfectly. This happens quite frequently. Edmund takes tours up to those ruins and they all forget to come home."

"What about a phone call?" Dorothy gave a nervous kind of cough.

"You see Mr. Lawrence, it was decided a long time ago not to put telephone lines up there. Parliament felt it would deface the sacred ruins of Camelot."

"I see." In the meantime Jack is pacing the floor looking a tad lost.

Grabbing for his office keys he says "Mr. Lawrence, are you still game for chess?"

"You must have read my mind."

"The game is right where we left it."

"It's been a long time since I've played."

"Why is that?"

"Just haven't found the time."

"Hi dad."

"Hey sport. What's going on?"

"Dad, the pool is huge."

"I know Joseph."

"Thanks Dad. I'm having the best time. Did Mom get back yet?"

"No, not yet."

"Ok, I'm going back to the pool. Tell me when she gets home."

The game lounge was quiet. At one table is a game of checkers. The other, some men playing pinochle, and there sat the chess game.

"Dorothy, would you care to stay?"

"Certainly, thank you."

"This game is beautiful."

"I am glad you think so. It is called Knights of the Round Table Chess."

"Gee, I wonder why."

The pieces were gold and red, silver and blue. The board was gold trimmed with a filigree design on all four corners. The squares were red and blue. A sommelier came to ask if any of them wished anything from the bar.

"Mr. Lawrence, would you care for a brandy, and you Dorothy?" All of them nodded yes.

"Three brandy's Brian."

Martin and Jack placed the pieces on the board. King, Queen, Bishop, Castle, Knight, Rook, and Pawn. Jack was simply mesmerized as to how these pieces looked so real.

"Let the games begin." Martin and Dorothy were pleased with what came from the game. Jack was unaware that Merlin had created the game as a connection to what was to be in both worlds. The only way the magic works is if the true guardian was in Arthur or Merlin's presence.

"Mr. Lawrence, what color do you choose?"

"Silver, Martin." Martin turned the silver side to Jack.

"I wish Arianna were here to watch this game."

"Why is that Mr. Lawrence?"

"Please, both of you, call me Jack."

"All right Jack. Why do wish Mrs. Lawrence to be here?" The sommelier brought the brandy snifters to the table.

"Dorothy, I promised Arianna I would teach her to play chess a long time ago. I never kept my promise, I kept forgetting."

"Tell me Jack, has your wife ever forgotten you?"

"No, not really."

"Mrs. Lawrence came all the way to England and ended up spending a day in the hospital with you for your needs. She could have been in the pool or taking a tour. After all, she'd only recently been in the hospital herself."

"How do you know?"

"We had a long talk about things, you know, woman to woman."

"Is that so?" Jack's voice was a little irritating.

"Jack, hum. Hum."

"Can we play Martin?"

"Yes of course." Dorothy now tries to get a last word in.

"You may not think so but a game of chess or even poker could be foreplay for a man and a woman." Jack had his mind on the board.

"Yeah, maybe."

"Jack, make your move." His move was the King piece. While removing the piece from the square, Martin and Dorothy could see Modred and his armies coming up the northeastern side of the lake. Martin therefore moved his castle piece. This square showed Merlin with Arthur. Dorothy sighed.

"What is wrong Dorothy?"

"Nothing Jack. Concentrate on the game." Jack moved his pawn and revealed Giles. He had been ordered ahead of Modred, hiding in the trees behind Percy and Ralph, listening to whatever he could bring back to Modred. Finally, Martin moved his Queen piece. There they viewed Lady Arianna and Galahad.

"Oh Thank God."

"Why did you say that?"

"Chess has always been a competitive game for me Mr. Lawrence. I find the moves quite the challenge."

The moves were played on. Dorothy and Martin were deduced with their connection with Merlin. One more piece was moved, Martin moved his Knight. As he moved it from square to square the piece made a tinny sound.

"Peter."

"My Lady."

"Please get my horse ready." Arianna felt Excalibur vibrate. It was time to leave.

"Can I come with you My Lady?"

"Galahad please stay here. You must realize Merlin brought me here for a reason."

Gawain took Arianna's hands in his.

"We know Arianna, we know." Galahad is now totally perplexed at this point.

"Merlin told us before he left to join Arthur. Your hands are shaking"

"Why did you not tell me?"

"To keep you safe."

"I understand." Catherine hugged and kissed Arianna while Peter brings Brach to Arianna fully equipped for her journey.

"Your horse My Lady."

"Thank you Peter."

Gawain helped Arianna to her horse. Gawain kissed her hand. As Sir Brach galloped away, Catherine shouted, "GOD GO WITH YOU!"

Holding Excalibur tight in her hand, Arianna rebutted "PLEASE, GOD GO WITH US."

Martin looked at his watch: Four hours to go.

Chapter Twenty-Two

MODRED'S TREACHERY

The sky has shown its hour of dusk.

"Stop Sir Brach. We will rest here." Dismounting, she realized this was the hill she was arrested on. She held on tight to Excalibur's hilt.

"Brach, I must be a fool. After Galahad asked me for Excalibur's assistance and she sang for him. They all realized I am her guardian. I should have known they knew. I guess I have been too preoccupied. I wish Merlin were here."

Brach made that snorting sound of his. Arianna acted on it, looking around. There was a cluster of pine trees and in the middle sat a man dressed in black and silver and another man dressed in the same armor stood next to him. Arianna moved ten feet closer straining to hear their conversation.

"My Lord, your fathers' camp is on the south side."

"The south side? Does he think The Lady of the Lake will help him? When I am King I will banish her from the Lake and give this to Mab as my gift for victory."

"Giles."

"Yes my Prince."

"Do you see the trees by the crest over there?"

"I see them my Prince."

"Place your men over there. Make no fires." Another man came.

"Pierce, take your men and place them at the edge of the lake." Pierce bowed his head, making ready to obey the command. Modred stood and placed his hands at his waist, sides bending at the elbows. His stance gave him a fallacy of power.

"When the North Star is at its brightest we will attack."

Arianna and Brach remained quiet behind the trees. Modred, Pierce and Giles hugged each other in vicious adulation.

"We must pour wine my Prince. By nights end you will be King."

"We must be quiet. Modred's men are moving."

It was getting dark. The stars were beginning to twinkle in the night's dome.

"Sir Brach, could those black eyes of yours see in the dark? Please help me find Merlin."

She mounted Brach. "Let us go!"

Arianna strained to see in front of her. Brach knew to walk quietly. Horse and rider were as one. Through the break in the vast trees Arianna could see a shimmer of lake. Brach knew his own by the sound of his breathing and the flicker of his mane they were on Arthur's side. They stopped to look around. Arianna scanned the dark. She could make out images while trying to recognize voices. She was so frightened it was hard to concentrate. In this confusing pool of darkness Arianna could make out a body form. She studied all her new friends so well she knew the shapes of their bodies in the dark. At least she hoped she did.

"Please God, let it be Merlin." It was getting too dark.

"If only I could find him. Brach what should I do? Should I tell him I am here or stay away. My heart tells me to go to him but I know better. I could change his history, my history, and Excalibur's. Arianna gave Brach a light kick to go up the hill.

"Thank God the moon is full. We will stay here. I hope this place will be safe."

"Dear God, shield us this night so I could help Merlin. Your will be done." While praying she dismounted Brach.

"You know my friend it is getting chilly." Taking a blanket from the saddlebag she sat next to a tree and covered herself. As time passed, her mind went back and forth from Arthur to Jack comparing both men. Arthur was a man who accepted his life and tried to go on where Jack had trouble accepting life's challenges putting up walls to hide behind. Yet she does love him and fought hard for both of them, all of them. Now she has to fight for Merlin. Could someone fight for her sometime?

Sometimes the loneliness wore its wounds too deep. The moonlight grew brighter. The wait felt like the times she spent in the hospital with Jack. The anxiety could kill a horse. Waiting for results. Waiting, waiting, an eternity of waiting. If Jack only knew somedays she hated his complacent illness and somedays it held her close to him. Her thoughts brought her into a twilight sleep. She awakened startled by a recurring nightmare: Joseph getting lost in a crowd, she's screaming, looking everywhere, but Joseph is nowhere to be found. The sound of an owl spooked Arianna. She checked the area making sure she was still safe.

Darkness had taken over. Vision was now difficult. Despite the inevitable, the night was filled with enchantment. The trees, the grass were all shades of indigo. As the moon took its light from the setting sun the white clouds glowed. The stars, especially the North Star, were so bright. Arianna could see the lake through the trees. It was a vision of moving lights. Hence the name "The City of Northern Lights." How could such beauty become a battleground?

"I wish I could make out Arthur's voice, Brach. We are too far away." Suddenly, there was a whipping kind of hissing sound. Arianna looked up, there were arrows heading right for Arthur's camp. Arrows lit with fire. Modred had made the first attack. Men screamed in pain. Then came the thunderous sound of horses running through the forest floor. Arianna could feel the vibration through her body. The muffled voices became clear.

"It is Modred." She could here Merlin's voice---"Thank God."
He was giving orders.
"Please God, help them."

The battle was hard to listen to. The clashes of metal on metal were earsplitting. From where she hid the moonlight gave reflection to swords waving, hitting lunging. Men fist fighting. She did not have to see the battle. The sounds were enough to feel death and despair all around. Arianna held on to Brach.

"Will I be brave enough to face this? I do not know."

Out of the noise she heard Arthur's voice shouting "FORWARD, SOUTH OF THE EMBANKMENT!"

The fiery arrows took to the sky again. The thunderous sound of horses galloping in battle mode and men running fearful of their lives. It was awful, spine tingling.

The spears shotputting through the air made an eerie whistling sound. Sir Brach became so scared he whinnied, snorted and to no avail, ran away. Arianna was now completely alone. She ran further up the hill, finding shelter behind twin maples. The battle continued all night. Neither side would retreat. Arianna did not have to see, she knew bodies lay everywhere. She could tell by the sound of voices in pain, swords struggling to fight, that the battle was weakening. Except for one battle. The North Star had begun to lose its brightness. Dawn was now evident—Anxiety was now mounding. This was it. Arianna paced. All she could do was hold on to Excalibur.

"Let us get the deed done. Dear God, how could I think such a thing? My God, what Merlin must be going through! Arthur, Dear God, Arthur, the fear of facing Modred! What goes through a man's mind when he has to face such an ordeal. This is Merlin's night. I have to concentrate on that." Arianna looked up to the scantly lit sky.

"Father in heaven, give us both the strength for whatever reason you have brought us together." The sounds of angry swords clashing broke whatever thoughts ran through Arianna.

"It is time Excalibur." Arianna fled to Merlin's side. The sound of swords grew louder, so did Arthur's voice become clearer. Arianna ran so fast down the hill she fell. She blindly lost her footing. When she got up, she realized she fell over Giles. He was dead, his breastplate split, stained with blood. She grabbed Excalibur and continued. The sights were devastating. What Arianna only imagined hours ago, were now in front of her. Death lay all around. The land Modred so eagerly wanted now was purchased with good men's blood. Modred had fallen another of Arthur's men.

"F-A-T-H-E-R."--- The shrill of his voice carried through the forest. Arthur did not answer. About one hundred yards away, Arthur sat on the ground, one of his men lay in his lap.

"A-R-T-H-U-R, W-H-E-R-E A-R-E Y-O-U!!?"

King Arthur tore off his helmet. Ralph lay in his lap. Ralph was the only one of Arthur's men to have red hair. Sir Ralph died in Arthur's loving arms. Hence Modred used the situation for his brutal attack. Modred struck Arthur on the back with a heavy branch. Arthur screamed in pain while wrenching his shoulder blades. Arthur stood weak. Again, Modred attacked with a blow to Arthur's face. Arthur wiped his face. His lower lip and cheek were bleeding.

"Why do you hate me so?"

"You bedded my mother and left her with me." Arthur stood emotionally paralyzed, trying not to fight his son. He bent down to pick up Excalibur. Again, Modred struck. This time, with his sword slashing Arthur's arm. Arthur's face had one question on it. Why?

"YOU DID NOT WANT ME, YOU WOULD NOT MARRY MOTHER!" Again, he lunged. Arthur swerved away.

"THAT IS NOT TRUE!"

"YOU LEFT ME A BASTARD!" Modred again lunged, this time Excalibur did the talking.

"I DID NOT KNOW YOU EXISTED! I FOUND OUT YEARS LATER!"

"YOU LIE AGAIN, FATHER." The swords clashed. Excalibur sang, but not like before. There was no honor or glory in her song this time.

Through all this mayhem, the sound of a horse galloping came through. It was Merlin. Merlin jumped off his horse and therefore drew his sword. Arthur yelled: "STAY OUT OF THIS!"

"But Sire…" Merlin desperately tries to distract Modred. Whoever was left alive from both armies surrounded Arthur, Modred and Merlin.

Arthur lunged at Modred, opening his shoulder. Both men ordered the men to retreat. Merlin drew back his sword. Their men by Merlin's example drew back. This was their fight. Arianna taking safe haven by an old oak tree stood horrified. There was nothing she could do. She held on to Excalibur. Suddenly her sword vibrated again, but this time there was no icy chill. She was hot, as though she too were fighting, maybe frightened. Modred swung, lunged and impaled Arthur right through his breastplate. Arthur paid no attention to the blood coming through the plate.

"YOUR MOTHER WANTED NOTHING TO DO WITH YOU OR ME. DEAR GOD MODRED, MORGANA WAS UNDER MAB'S SPELL! MODRED, PLEASE. MAB COULD NOT CONTROL ME OR MY MAGIC SO SHE PUT LIES IN YOUR HEAD!"

"MERLIN, SHUT UP. I WILL HEAR NOTHING FROM YOU!" Modred kept swinging, pushing Merlin down.

"Merlin are you…"

"I am alright, Arthur!"

"ARTHUR!!" Modred jumped on top of Arthur. Arthur fought him off. When rising his breastplate fell off. Arthur was now completely consumed with anger. He pushed Modred into a tree from the back.

"I HAVE HAD ENOUGH. I AM YOUR FATHER AND YOU WILL HEAR ME!!"

"HEAR YOU?" Modred's nose was now bleeding.

"NO FATHER, NOW HEAR THIS." Modred impaled Arthur's chest.

"ARTHUR, NO-O-O!" Merlin cried out while Arthur was falling to his knees.

Modred, confident Arthur was now completely weak, put his guard down. Watching, watching, Arthur holding his wound, blood gushing to his hand. Arthur, with shock on his face and anger now in his heart, stood with the help of Excalibur.

With Arthur's last ounce of energy: "MODRED!" Modred laughed insanely at Arthur's weakness. His evil face dares him. Go ahead. Arthur angrily impales Modred straight through. He then drew back Excalibur. Modred fell to his knees with disbelief on his face, holding the gushing wound, took one last look at Arthur, keeled over and died. Modred's men fled quickly.

Arthur himself then fell giving into his wounds. Looking at his son Modred's lifeless body Arthur mournfully streamed tears, unimaginable tears. "Modred— Modred my son." Merlin ran to Arthur while Arianna just stood, watching, her legs paralyzed from this trauma she had witnessed. She so wanted to go to both of them, but she knew these were their last private moments together. Merlin sat on the ground, picked Arthur up and gently held him in his loving arms. Arthur's chest was so badly wounded, his tunic soaked in blood. Merlin tried covering the wound with a cloth, but his desperate hands could not stop it.

Arthur's face was so ashen, his breathing labored.

"My son, I am so sorry." Disparity was written on Merlin's face.

"Forgive me. In trying to keep peace in my own life, I have given you pain."

Death's reign now befell Arthur's face.

"Merlin, I did love Modred." King Arthur, laboring to speak.

"My soul wi---ill never have pe---ace. Please God forgive me. For---forgive Mo ---Modred.

Sir Frederick and Sir William painfully watched on. Arianna overheard Sir William say, "How will we live without King Arthur?" Sir Frederick put his hand on William's shoulder, then rested his weary head on top and said "I do not know my brother, but we must find Percy and John."

Arthur lay safe in Merlin's arms, holding onto Merlin's cloak with one hand and Excalibur with the other. Holding onto life for as long as he could. Knowing that his life was at an end, he said these words to his foster father: "Merlin I love you." Tears fell on Merlin's cheek.

"Tell Galahad, he is my pride and joy." Merlin, holding Arthur tighter in his arms.

"He knows Sire, he knows.' Arthur now holds on harder, laboring.

"Cath –erine, tell Arian –a, I love her." Arianna fell to her knees, doubled over in grief.

"No God, No!"

Arthur looked up to Merlin and let go of his Spirit.

"ARTHUR PENDRAGON, KING OF CAMELOT" was dead of fatal wounds. Merlin folded Arthur's body in his arms, then cried bitterly in his chest. Arthur's men knelt before their King.

"Please make your way. Let us alone." William gave the signal to leave. Merlin transfixed on Arthur, started rocking his body gently as though a babe in arms. Merlin's sullen voice whispered quietly to Arthur's still body.

"Oh my son, My King it should be me lying in your arms. The elder should bury the younger. I brought you to this. I wanted a good man to be king and I got one. But what price to pay. My Sweet King, in this forever, sleep, sleep well." Merlin kept rocking silently, rocking the morning chill, and covering him as though a blanket.

"NO, DEAR GOD, NO!!" His lamenting cries filled the forest. Arianna kept careful watch. Merlin grabbed for Arthur's lifeless hand and instead held onto Excalibur's blade, cutting his finger. He looked at the cut, laughing morosely.

"Excalibur, You! YOU and THE LADY OF THE LAKE promised me you would protect Arthur! YOU DID NOT KEEP YOUR PROMISE. Instead, you brought destruction to him. I HATE YOU BOTH FOR THIS!"

Merlin sat and kept rocking Arthur in a kind of maddening silence. Arianna knew not what to do. She wanted to take the pain from Merlin, but she knew this was impossible. Pulling Arthur's clasped hand from his cloak, he gently laid his King on the ground, and rose to his feet. Taking off his cloak he folded it and placed it under Arthur's head. He then knelt down and kissed Arthur on the forehead. Merlin had a quiet anger about him, the worst kind of anger. A man of faith could be blinded by such anger, such anguish.

Modred lay a few steps away. He walked over and in some weary way rolled Modred's body over. He then bent over stroking his cheek, whispering, "You will never be King my boy." Standing quickly his body ever so ridged. His hands, clenched, as though ready to fight the world.

Merlin frightfully screamed "A-R-E Y-O-U H-A-P-P-Y M-A-B? Look Mab, NO ONE W-I-N-S. NO ONE! My magic, your magic, could not save either one of them. Where are you MAB?"

Mab never showed herself. Merlin again screamed: "LADY OF THE LAKE, WHERE ARE YOU?" There was no answer. His anger swelled.

"THE MAGIC'S GONE. ALL IS GONE. MY LIFE, ARTHUR'S LIFE has had no meaning. Then the ONE thing left from magic and I will rid the world of her: E-X-C-A-L-I-B-U-R!!"

Merlin ran with great haste to Arthur's body, ripping Excalibur from Arthur's hand.

"LADY OF THE LAKE, if you are there…" Arianna knew this was it.

"MERLIN NO!!" Arianna's voice ripped shockingly through the forest floor as she ran to the lake.

"TAKE HER BACK LADY!!" Merlin had Excalibur in both hands. He was about to throw her in the lake, when Arianna lunged in front of him. Merlin, horrified, stopped short. He almost struck Arianna fatally with Excalibur. The maddening look in Merlin's eyes frightened Arianna.

"GET AWAY FROM ME!!"

Arianna now acting with caution says: "No, you brought me here to help you." Merlin pushed Arianna to the ground. Arianna's face cringed, her lower back now in pain.

Arianna picked herself up, as Merlin was shotputting Excalibur to the water. Arianna stopped him with her Excalibur. As the two swords crossed the sound vibrated through the lake. Arianna's eyes pierced Merlin's.

"Do not make the same mistake twice. I cannot stop you but I will surely try!" The two of them had frozen in the same stance, not giving in to each other.

"You do not understand Arianna, I caused this. Arthur, Modred, all that you see is my fault." Merlin again attempts the deed but Arianna foils his efforts. She reaps at his Excalibur. The swords clash is even louder.

"You brought me here to help you. LET ME MERLIN, PLEASE!"

"Listen to me, first put Excalibur down, as will I." Merlin looked into Arianna's determined eyes and finally put Excalibur down on the grass with hers.

"All your soul has suffered is not your doing. Arthur, Modred, this is their fate not yours. You have punished yourself for something even your magic could not control. Merlin now looking completely engulfed in his emotion tries to find some sanity in the situation.

"How did you know when to come, Arianna," realizing he is taking control of his senses.

"Excalibur told me. She has been giving me signals the whole time I have been here. All night listening, watching."

"All night, where?" Arianna points up the hill.

"There, over the hill behind the twin maples."

Merlin looking around at the after outcome of this scene of battle, with a befuddled expression says: "How is it you are unharmed?"

Arianna now fully internalizes the bloody scene, which has been placed before her, and rebuts the question. "I do not know, all I can say is God must have sheltered me as he sheltered you."

"Sheltered me?" As he points to himself.

"I just watched my son die."

Merlin fell to his knees and picked up Excalibur saying "Excalibur could not save Arthur, so why should I save her?" Arianna knelt down with Merlin.

"I just realized where we are. This is your purgatory, Merlin. Please let go. Forgive yourself."

Arianna took both Excalibur's and crossed them on the ground. Merlin buried his face in his hands. Arianna watched this man of great strength cry a lamenting cry he waited so long to release. As he cried Excalibur's body and soul became one again. She sang her beautiful song of dignity.

"Look Merlin, Excalibur is one again. We did it." Merlin reaches for his beautiful Excalibur, now realizing that he almost threw her away.

"Thank you my dear sweet friend." Arianna brushed Merlin's hair from his face.

"My friend, it is I who thank you. You helped me realize that all I have been through has not been my fault, some things I cannot change either."

With these words of friendship they held each other. Out of the dead calm came a beautiful voice: "Merlin, Arianna." They both looked up.

"Merlin look, your aunt, The Lady of the Lake." Her weightless body hovered over the lake, taking careful note as to the senselessness of lives lost.

"You have done well both of you. Bring Excalibur to me."

Merlin's eyes gazed at the beautiful sword in his hand then gave it to his aunt.

"My dear Lady, Excalibur looks as she did the day you gave her to me." Merlin carefully places Excalibur in his aunts' hands. She then looks at Arianna.

"Arianna, you are to choose an heir." Arianna realizes Merlin is not allowed to choose Excalibur's heir. His mistake took that honor away from him.

Arianna humbly asks: "May I have Excalibur, My Lady of the Lake?" The Lady gave the sword to Arianna. Arianna then walked over to King Arthur's body. It was now her turn to pay her respects to her fallen friend. Trying to hold back tears, Arianna knelt before Arthur.

"Dear God, there is so much blood." She beckoned Merlin, come kneel with her. Merlin knelt down, looking dazed. He was with his dear friends, both of them.

Arianna placed Excalibur across Arthur's chest, taking his lifeless hand in hers whispering softly: "Excalibur belongs to you my sweet, sweet King, my Friend. With your most royal permission I will give Excalibur to Galahad."

Then finally her strength gave way. The tears bitterly showed themselves. Arianna buried her face in Arthur's waist and sobbed. This time Merlin held Arianna's shaking body. The Lady watched on then wrapped her beautiful dress around them to comfort both of them. Then she spoke to them saying; "Your choice is wise Arianna. I am pleased."

Merlin helped Arianna to her feet.

"My Lady, do you know if my family is well?"

"They are Arianna, Sir Martin and Lady Nimue keep close watch on them."

"Do they know I am missing?"

"Not yet, but time is of an essence right now."

"My Lady please, my wife, is she well?"

"Nimue is quite well."

"The chess set. Did it work?" The Lady smiled with pride at her nephew.

"A game of great wisdom." Merlin shook his head in agreement.

"I am glad it worked."

Arianna then asks Merlin: "What chess set?"

"I will explain on our way home. It is time we return to Camelot."

"My Lady, may I stay for His Majesty's burial rights?"

"My child, your work is not yet finished. Give the sword to Galahad, hence leave at the first light of the North Star. You will be escorted safely."

Arianna walks back over to the lake, kneels at the edge of the water washing her face with the crisp blue water, then looks up to the Lady and asks: "Will I ever see you again?"

The Lady comes closer to Arianna and Merlin. She strokes Arianna on the cheek, then answers the question.

"In some way, we will meet again, I promise."

The Lady kissed Merlin and Arianna good-bye and vanished into the lake. Arthur's two remaining Knights came from the embankment. Arianna and Merlin watched them come forward. Sir William dismounted first and tenderly greeted Arianna with a kiss on the hand then saluted Merlin with his sword, as did Frederick follow.

"We found your horse, My Lady."

"Sir Brach, you..." Arianna covered her face with both hands.

"My God in Heaven" was her response. Brach was carrying Sir John and Sir Percy's bodies. Arianna went to their aid while they took their bodies off her horse. She caressed Brach gently on his neck.

"I am so sorry. What can I do to help?" Arianna bent down near John and Percy making the Sign of the Cross. Then the quiet tears came.

"Merlin, Arthur's horse is tied over there." Merlin acknowledged and untied him. Merlin mounted Julius. Sir Frederick helped Lady Arianna on Brach, then handed Excalibur to her for safe keeping.

"My Lady we are sorry we doubted you."

"It is alright my friends, I understand."

Arthur's precious body was given to Merlin to carry back to Camelot. Sir William carried John's body and Sir Frederick carried Ralph's. Bennett took Sir Percy's body.

Sir William then led the funeral procession back to Camelot. Riding away, Arianna looked back at this now place of death, asking one question.

"William."

"My Lady?"

"What will happen to the bodies?"

"We will send a group to retrieve them."

"And Modred?"

"He will be buried somehow."

Chapter Twenty-Three

EXCALIBUR'S HEIR

The procession out of the forest was quiet. As they approached the bridge into the city, all could hear Camelot's heart was broken. For they already knew the fate of their King and their loved ones.

Sir William stepped aside so that Merlin with King Arthur could take the lead. Galahad took notice that Merlin was riding Sir Julius. Young Galahad and Young Peter stood at the front gate dressed in Knights uniforms. A full Honor Guard awaited Arthur. As the gate opened Arthur's young soldiers guarded the wall up above the square. The others stood at least thirty on each side for an arched sword salute. All that was heard were the sound of the horses' hooves. By the time they reached the castle steps the mourning began. Sir Gawain stood in full dress armor. Lady Catherine and Lady Nimue stood at either side. When Merlin saw Nimue his eyes filled. His wife made it home to be with him. Sir Gawain honored King Arthur, then took his body from Merlin. Sir Ralph and Sir John and finally Sir Percy's wives were there to claim their spouses.

Catherine and Arianna hugged each other in a way sisters hold on when they both feel the same pain.

"My dear, are you alright?"

Arianna held onto Excalibur for strength answering "I will be alright Catherine, I just need some rest."

Catherine went back to her husband's side. The whole scene was a vast space of emotional confusion. A blanket was placed on the steps for Arthur's body to lay upon. Young Galahad and young Peter were the first to order a salute for their King. Then, being young men broke down at the sight of their fallen King. Sir William came to the aid of his son Peter and Galahad.

Arianna stood to the side. She was there alone and alone she would remain. Her mind clouded by the trauma she had witnessed. Why now were there no tears? Her mission was done. "One thing was left, give Excalibur to Galahad." She quickly thought: "Not now, we have to bury Arthur my friend first." Arianna had too many thoughts at once. The sight of Merlin and Nimue together pleased Arianna's heart. Merlin needed Nimue right now. His heart carried a heavy burden. Arthur and his Knights were brought into the castle. Their bodies would be prepared for their funerals in the morning. Nimue and Merlin made their way towards Arianna.

"Lady Arianna."

"Oh Merlin."

"This is my wife..."

"I know, Nimue."

Arianna had already put two and two together. If Edmund was Merlin, then Dorothy was surely Nimue.

"Thank you for helping my husband."

"Please, I am the one who is honored." Nimue gazes down at Excalibur in her sheath.

"My Lady, may I see Excalibur?" Arianna drew her forth. Nimue's eye opened wide and said: "She is magnificent, Merlin. It is no wonder the Lady sent you searching."

"I know my dear," and he kissed his wife tenderly on the cheek.

"Arianna, keep her safe."

"I promise, dear Merlin." Arianna started walking away.

"Lady Arianna?"

"Sir Gawain."

"May we see you in quarters?"

"Certainly, right away."

"May we follow Sir Gawain?"

"My dear ladies, you are the spouses of Arthur's cherished Knights. All are invited to the "Round Table." It is Arthur's wish." As he said these words, he choked back tears. Sir Gawain led the procession into the room.

"Please, be seated." Merlin, Nimue, and Arianna sat in what once was a treasured member of Arthur's court.

This once Hallowed room felt Hollow without the presence of Arthur and his men.

Catherine poured wine for all seated. When she served Arianna, she stared at Arianna's dress, then at Merlin's tunic. There were not any words spoken. The battle was evident on their clothes. Merlin then stood from his chair, taking his place near Arianna. Gawain now lit the torch on the main wall, turned, and looked at Arianna.

"My Lady, may we have EXCALIBUR for His Lordships burial rights?"

Arianna sat there in kind of a haunting silence. Looking down, her dress stained with Arthur's blood, her mind tired. For what felt like forever she had been caretaker of the most famous of all swords. Now she was being asked to render her over. Excalibur and Arianna had become one for a while, returning her to history is now a difficult task. The Lady Arianna stood, took a sip of wine, then drew Excalibur from her sheath. She then placed Excalibur on Arthur's chair. For she returned her to her owner one last time. The fire lit in the middle of the table gave Excalibur an eerie glow.

"William, Merlin could you tell us?" Merlin stood, while removing his sword. All eyes were fixed on him.

"I know what you want to hear. Modred is dead."

The room burst into: "AMEN!"

Merlin sat back down quietly. Lord Gresham, one of Arthur's men at court replied: "Is that all you have to say?" William's angry green eyes stared at Gawain and Gresham.

"Do you wish to know how he died?" Gawain folded his arms in front of him and paced the floor.

"Of course I want to know how." William pounded his fist on the table.

"Dear God Man, by the hand of King Arthur! And King Arthur by the hand of Modred!"

Arianna buried her face in her hands and said: "It was awful." Then by acknowledgement, she touched Arthur's blood on her dress. The room fell silent.

Sir William put his arm around Peter. Peter was surprised by the gesture. Sir William then said: "My son, I will Love and cherish you forever."

Galahad became so viciously angry. He yelled "What has come of all this? I have lost two fathers. There is no joy left in my heart. When father's and sons show malice to each other, how can there be peace anywhere!"

He then blindly took his dagger from its belt and threw it across the room. Ironically it landed right under the crucifix Arthur himself made by hand. Galahad took it as an omen and quieted himself.

Friar Thomas entered the room. A tall man with shoulder length white hair, dressed in black and gray. He addressed Sir Gawain about the funeral arrangements. Sir Gawain re-entered the room, heading straight for Merlin.

"Merlin, may I speak with you?" Merlin moved towards Sir Gawain.

"Friar Thomas wishes to be told who will be the heir to Excalibur."

"Lady Arianna, Friar Thomas wishes to know who is Excalibur's Noble Heir."

Arianna's brown eyes connected with Merlin's silver blue eyes and said: "I CHOOSE GALAHAD."

Galahad startled by the decision answered: "I AM NOT WORTHY OF SUCH A BLESSING."

Friar Thomas beckoned Galahad to come to him. He placed both hands on Galahad's shoulders, gazed into Galahad's blue eyes, and replied: "Son, you have been given a noble gift. It is your decision to accept it. Search your heart, by light of morn give me your answer."

Arianna's heart began to race as she reached for Merlin's hand.

"I do not understand Merlin, why did he not accept Excalibur?"

"My Lady, because Galahad is so young he must make the decision on his own. The responsibility is a great one." Arianna nodded her head in agreement.

"Then we must hurry and pray he accepts."

"Yes Arianna, we must."

A young galley boy entered the room announcing the main meal was served. The day had passed so quickly. It was already late noon.

Chapter Twenty-Four

KING ARTHUR'S FUNERAL

Camelot did not sleep this night. In those days, funerals such as this one took long hours of preparation. Many torches lit the Village Square. Arthur will be given a Viking funeral. The bed of firewood and kindling where he will lay for cremation had to be built in proper proportion. The women in the castle worked all night to make ready the funeral attire. Black and purple were the colors of choice.

Arianna had never seen such preparations. For her mothers and brothers funerals all she did was appear in church dressed properly. Here all is involved. This was Arthur's wish that all his people live and work in harmony. King Arthur paid the most expensive price of all for his dream.

A hot bath felt good after the ordeal that was behind all that survived. After her bath Arianna darned a dressing gown. She stood on her verandah. There she could see the preparations. The Cathedral would be too small for all of Camelot to attend. Friar Thomas and his fellow priests were busy setting up the altar outside. The lifelike Crucifix with the torchlight's shining on it made Jesus appear somewhat eerie. A chill ran up Arianna's spine. You could not help but think that a wedding might be taking place. The colors and the moral proved otherwise. While standing out there, for some reason a tune from a movie she saw kept playing in her head. She could not remember the words but it had something to do about how the heart hurts when loved ones are lost. Her thoughts were interrupted by a knock on the door. Arianna went to answer it.

"Galahad, what are you doing here?"

"Sir William sent me to talk with you." His hands were shaking.

"Are you alright?"

"No, not really." Galahad takes a chair near the fireplace.

"Why did you choose me?" Arianna realizes Galahad is petrified.

"I chose you because of how you felt when King Arthur took you in. God rest him. Because for a young man, you are honest with your feelings. I chose you because you forgave your father for leaving you and for the death of your mother."

Galahad put a cord of wood in the low burning fire.

"My Lady you are wrong. When I first came here I hated being here. I never told anyone this but I hated His Majesty for banishing my father. I blamed him for my mother's death." Arianna sees the pain Galahad has buried down deep. She caresses his cheek. Galahad then holds Arianna's hand close to his face; he cradles in the warmth of her touch.

"It took me a long time to find forgiveness for all of them. Peter hated me."

"Why did Peter hate you?"

Galahad chuckles, then says: "I would put dead rodents in his bed."

Arianna is surprised yet nauseated at the same time.

"Dear Lord, what for?"

"He had two parents who loved him. I was jealous."

"Oh, I see. What happened to Peter's mother?"

"Dear God, Lady Helen died of lung disease. She was so beautiful."

"How old was Peter?"

"He was twelve. I was thirteen."

"My goodness that was five years ago."

Galahad then exits the room to sit on the verandah, staring at the preparations. Arianna follows.

"How did you find forgiveness?"

"As I got older, Friar Thomas explained how important a marriage is between a man and a woman and how my father Lancelot and Queen Guenevere defaced and mocked their marriage vows. I realized Uncle Arthur was merciful."

"How mature of you then."

Galahad turns, folds his arms in front of him and says: "Not maturity, reality My Lady. My father killed my beautiful mother and a piece of Arthur also. Seems as though everyone has taken a piece of Uncle Arthur. I hate Modred." Arianna rubs his forearm trying to comfort him.

"You will forgive him someday."

"ENOUGH! Why did you not choose Sir Gawain or Sir William? They have the wisdom of the years behind them." Galahad's forlorn eyes look deeply into Arianna's for answers.

"Galahad, Excalibur sang in your hands. She already knows to whom her service belongs. Please open your heart."

Galahad grabbed Arianna's hand, opened the door and literally dragged her down the hall. Galahad pushed open Arthur's chamber doors. He then lit the wall torch. Arthur's room seemed like a sanctuary. There was an eerie feeling of peace. Arthur's clothes had been laid out on the bed. He will wear his red velvet shirt for his funeral. His black boots polished. His black over tunic with the Pendragon symbol and the sword with a gold formei cross in the dragons' hand was neatly placed with it. Arthur's scabbard belt and scabbard sat on the bench. Arthur's crown, a simple gold band with small onyx and a red stone in the front was carefully placed on the pillow. Galahad was ashamed he had burst in as he did.

"You see, this is why I cannot carry Excalibur. I cannot be like Uncle Arthur nor am I ready to be the Lord of Camelot or live in this room!" Arianna walks about the room and answers Galahad in this way.

"Galahad, no one is asking you to be like King Arthur. You will mold the position to your liking not Arthur's. You had to have known that Arthur would have wished for you to follow him. Your heart and your mind must have told you, maybe even warned you. Please realize you were chosen for who you are."

Galahad is nervously pacing the room examining His Majesty's clothes.

Galahad then rebuts with these words of honesty: "I am trying to understand you but I cannot promise miracles. We better leave, we should not be here when the priests come for Arthur's clothes." Arianna shakes her head in agreement.

"You are right Galahad." They went back to Arianna's room.

"Galahad, do you know why Arthur kept his wedding rings out even when…"

"Please do not say it."

"I am so sorry."

"No, listen. Gawain told me that Arthur left them there as an open reminder of a lost love. And how because of that he made a mistake with Morgana and that brought Modred. It reminded him not to make mistakes and never to judge people by appearances alone. A hard reminder every day." Now Arianna has a forlorn look in her eyes.

"Dear, Dear God."

"You know, I am hungry."

"You must be kidding. You are a typical boy, I mean young man. My children could eat me out of house and home."

"What do you mean?"

"Forget it. Come on, let us go to the galley." There were not any clocks around but Arianna assumed it must have been around ten o'clock P.M. She was tired and in desperate need of some sleep.

Galahad and Arianna walked into what she called: "Organized chaos." A wonderful smell of bread baking filled her nostrils. Buttermilk churned and fruits prepared for breakfast. There would not be any time in the morning for such preparations.

Galahad and Arianna asked for some bread and buttermilk then took their plates with them.

"Galahad, you have a few short hours to give Friar Thomas and myself an answer."

Fear returned to Galahad's face. He answered: "I know."

"Well, I suggest you eat that, go back to your room and think this through. I am tired. I have not slept in nearly two days. I do not wish to get sick again."

"Please stay with me."

"Galahad you must do this alone. You must decide this without influence of others, especially me. Now go please." Galahad was reluctant to leave.

" Good Night My Lady. You know it is times like these that I miss my mother."

Arianna strokes Galahad on the forearm.

"I know, so do I miss my mother. Now go." Arianna kissed Galahad on the cheek. Galahad walked away, taking Arianna's bread and buttermilk. In his room he ate again. Galahad always eats when he is nervous. Peter lays sound asleep. They shared a room since they were boys. When Galahad came to Camelot, Peter became his roommate so the transition would be less painful. The hours passed slowly. Fatigue set in and a prayer came from it.

"Dear God please help me. I know you have given me
a Great honor. Help me accept it."

Looking down at Peter, his stomach growing tight, he whispers:

"I am so afraid. I do not know how to be a leader. How
Jesus can you turn this boy into a man in just a few hours?
Uncle Arthur said I was not ready to fight with him. How
can I fight for this? How can I? I do not know."

"My hands, they are so cold." He started rubbing his hands together when his ring fell off. It was gold with a red stone in the middle, a gift from Arthur. Galahad sobbed, awakening Peter. Peter got up from his bed to sit with Galahad and therefore help his brother make this heartfelt decision.

Peter draped his arm around Galahad's shoulder and said these precious words: "I promise you my brother, I will pledge my allegiance to you as I did to His Majesty, King Arthur." Both young men hugged in bittersweet joy.

Peter stood and saluted Galahad with a closed fist to his heart. Galahad knew God had made the decision for him.

"Come brother, we must tell Friar Thomas and Lady Arianna."

"No brother, this is your honor. Take it. Go quickly!"

Galahad ran down the hall straight to Arianna's room, he gently opened the door.

"My Lady, please wake up." Shaking Arianna at the shoulder.

"Wake up, please!" Arianna sat up.

"What time is it?" Galahad pulled the curtain back. It was dawn.

"I am on my way to Friar Thomas but I came to see you first. I could not sleep all night. It was hard to decide but I know Uncle Arthur would have been proud to see this for me." Galahad took a deep breath.

"What I am trying to say is I will accept Excalibur."

"Thank you God" and she kissed Galahad on the cheek.

"Come with me to tell Friar Thomas."

"I will be happy to." Arianna put on her robe and hence they walked the halls.

Galahad and Arianna knocked on the priest sanctuary door. Galahad looked pale. A young boy answered.

"Could you please tell Friar Thomas that Lady Arianna and Galahad are here." Friar Thomas entered the room looking straight at Galahad.

"Are you well my son?"

"I think so. I mean, I am not sure Good Father, I am terrified."

"It is good that you are. What say you?"

Galahad reached for strength in Arianna's eyes. He transfixed them to hers and said: "My good priest, I will accept guardianship of Excalibur." Friar Thomas realizes Galahad is taking strength from Arianna.

"Are you sure my son?" Galahad is trying to relax himself.

"If God is asking me through Lady Arianna then I must accept."

"A young man of faith. It is a good trait in a future leader."

"My Lady."

"Good Father."

"We have much to plan in a short time."

"I understand." Arianna knew Galahad and Friar Thomas needed time to be alone. It was already six A.M.

"If you need me, come or send for me."

Arianna went to hug Galahad. He was trembling. Walking back to her room Arianna could smell food. She was another one who could eat when she got nervous. She had been through enough funerals to know to eat to keep up with her strength.

By the time Arianna reached her room the sun was shining beautifully. A chamber girl helped her get into her black velvet dress. It was decorated with purple piping at the collar cuffs and hemline. There were purple ties for the back and the cuffs and a purple sash for the waist. As beautiful as it looked it was depressing to wear. Arianna stood outside on her verandah. The sight she saw last night was nothing compared to the daylight. The cremation bed was ready. The altar candles and colors adorned the square. All that was needed is the guest of honor.

After breakfast, Arianna stepped outside the castle. The children were being children, playing and singing. Could they comprehend any of this?

"Arianna… There you are!"

"Catherine, I do not have to ask you how you are."

"Dear God, can you believe all of this? Arianna I – I wish…" Catherine buried her face in her shawl weeping. "Why Arthur, why John, dear God why Ralph and Percy?" Arianna rubbed her back to try and comfort her. Today there would be no comfort. All felt this tragedy, all grieved.

Unlike Ralph, John and Percy, King Arthur did not have any family representation. He would have no parents or siblings, not anyone. There would not be any Dignitaries or Kings or Presidents. His Dignitaries are his Knights, his diplomats his people. This was Arthur's legacy.

The square started to fill with people. Those who could attend were from every class. There were those who owned farms, blacksmiths, weaponry smiths and armor makers. All were invited. Arthur welcomed rich and poor at all times. This is why Arthur was loved by all.

Merlin's heart was so full this day. He and Nimue joined the castle staff. He looked like a king himself. He wore a purple velvet shirt with a high funnel collar. The shirt was adorned by a gold leaf design on the sleeves and tasses. He had black velvet pants with high black boots. A black cape adorned all with the same gold leaf design around the border and down the middle. A mourning hood completed the cape. To complete his attire he wore a gold sheath belt and his dress gold sword, given to him by Arthur. He looked magnificent.

"My Lady."

"Good morning, Sir William."

"May I escort you?"

"It will be an honor."

The pages were scurrying about lighting torches. Arthur loved when torches lighted the square. Arthur's armies were up on the fort wall looking down protecting such a grand array of people. The tower bell rang a somber ring, one ring. One bell – a call to mass. Two bells for the priests' entrance. Four bells – Four bells, one for Sir Ralph, one for Sir John, one for Sir Percy and one bell and a horn fanfare for King Arthur.

Friar Thomas and Father James came down the stairs first, along with six young altar boys. Twelve young soldiers were chosen to carry the bodies of Sir John, Sir Ralph and Sir Percy. The burden was a great one but the way they carried themselves and their admired comrades, showed how revered the honor was. When their bodies were placed in front of the altar, the lamenting cries of their wives reminded Arianna of when she herself cried at her mothers' death. All around in one way or another one could hear these words: "Why them? They were good men. How could this have happened?"

A bell was heard coming from the cathedral tower signaling King Arthur's arrival. Three altar boys took the lead-two with candles lit and one with a small bell on which he rang one bell for each step taken. Peter and Galahad led the poles for Arthur. In back were Sir Frederick and Sir Gawain.

"Dear God Merlin, why is Galahad there? He should be preparing."

"I know My Lady, Galahad chose to honor Arthur first."

The men were all dressed in the finest of armor. Arthur lay on a board of wood draped in black, red and gold silk sheets. Arthur was dressed in red and black. The monotone bell was sombering. As Arthur drew closer to the altar Merlin dared to take notice as to how Friar Thomas crossed Arthur's hands at his chest holding precious Excalibur. He reached for Nimue's hand and Arianna's. Merlin kissed both their hands and said theses tender words: "It seems as though he is sleeping. I hope he has finally found peace with God and Modred." They all embraced each other.

The bell in the tower sounded the beginning of mass. Father James made the sign of the cross. The Gloria's and the Hosanna's were all prayed. The readings were Arthur's favorites, "The Good Samaritan" and "The Parable of the Prodigal Son." "The Liturgy of the Eucharist" was touching.

Father Thomas spoke of Sir Ralph, Sir Percy and Sir John's lives, and their bravery and of their goodness as men and family men.

He now spoke of His Majesty King Arthur. He told about the kind of man he was and how lightly he wore his crown. He spoke of Modred and how Arthur fought his battles as father and King to this boy. While Friar Thomas spoke Father James escorted Galahad and Peter back to the castle. Father James had everything ready. Galahad's breastplate and an empty sheath were set on the table. Father James became concerned when he saw Galahad's face grow pale again.

"Son, you are shaking." Galahad looked at the Good Father.

"It will not stop, my heart, my chest are throbbing."

Father began fastening the plate belts and said: "It will. God will help you. Both of you."

Peter's hands were shaking, sweating. He looked at Galahad saying, "I cannot believe this is happening. Could I ask-what are we all thinking?" James laughed and poured a glass of wine for each of them.

"Here, it will take the edge off." They all drank down.

Galahad looked like a king in full dress and Arthur's blue and gold cape. Peter wore a breastplate and a blue cape as well. Father James girded Galahad's sheath belt at his waist. The young men were ready. Galahad took one more sip of wine and said with readiness: "Let us go."

Father James rang one bell. Then escorted Galahad and Peter to the altar. Sir William stood amazed and baffled.

"Dear God, he has chosen Peter to be his First Knight. Merlin did you know any of this?"

"Not at all Sir William. It is a surprise to me also."

The young men stood at the altar. Father James asked Galahad: "Do you, Galahad come of your own choice?"

His answer: "I DO, GOOD FATHER."

"And you Peter, do you come of your own choice?"

His answer: "I DO ALSO, GOOD FATHER."

The men were instructed to kneel. Father James then blessed four small cruets of oil. By Christian law, the bodies are blessed with Holy Oils to purify the body to allow safe passage of the soul into Heaven. He blessed Ralph, John, Percy and then Arthur, each man with his own cruet. Each man's head, hands and lips were blessed: "IN THE NAME OF THE FATHER, AND OF THE SON, AND OF THE HOLY GHOST."

The people answered: "AMEN!"

Galahad was instructed to stand. Father James asked: "Galahad, do you reject all that is evil and take all that is good to your heart and soul?"

His answer: "I DO, GOOD FATHER."

Father Thomas went to Arthur's body, knelt in respect and removed his ring, giving it over to Father James.

"Galahad, I ask you, do you accept this ring as a token of leadership?"

Again his answer: "I DO, GOOD FATHER."

The beautiful gold and ruby ring was placed on Galahad's shaky right hand. Galahad then walked over to Arthur's body and kissed him gently on the face and hand. Friar Thomas now instructed Peter to stand. He asked Peter: "Do you Peter, reject all that is evil and take all that is good to your heart and soul?"

Peter answered: "I DO, GOOD FATHER."

Galahad then took off his ring; the one Arthur had given to him and placed it on Peter's shaky right hand. Galahad then asked Peter: "Do you Peter, swear to take this very sword as my First Knight?"

Peter answered with pride: "I DO, MY LORD."

Friar Thomas handed Galahad a gold and silver sword. Peter knelt down before Galahad. He then placed the sword in his trusting hands. Peter was surprised. It was the sword King Arthur gave Galahad for his eighteenth birthday.

Peter then rose to his feet and knelt down before the altar. Sir William could not fight tears-his son, what an honor. Lady Catherine stood next to him. Words were not spoken. The eyes told of pride on this day.

Peter dared to turn around to look at his father. Peter's shoulder was twitching. It always did when he found himself in tight places. This was Galahad's finest hour. Friar Thomas beckoned Galahad to approach the altar. Asking one more time: "Do you Galahad, come here of your own free will to receive the sword of Leadership?"

Galahad dared look at Arianna and with confidence said: "I WILL ACCEPT EXCALIBUR AS THE SWORD AND SYMBOL OF MY LEADERSHIP."

Friar Thomas and Father James blessed the Holy Oils and Anointed Galahad with the Sign of the Cross. First they blessed his head asking God for Spiritual Guidance. Then his shoulders were blessed asking God for strength to carry on in his leadership. The Sign of the Cross was put on each hand to ask God's help to build a strong foundation for Camelot and himself. Then Galahad's legs were blessed asking God to keep him steadfast and strong through all of life's endeavors. Then they blessed his lips in order for him to ask God to help him find the wisdom and courage that he will need in his office. The Sign of the Cross was placed on his heart asking God to keep him pure.

Friar Thomas walked over to Arthur asking: "Dear God through death you release Arthur of all his Kingly duties. Take him home in Heaven and give him peaceful reward."

All Shouted: "AMEN!"

Friar Thomas now withdrew Excalibur from King Arthur's hands. Arianna and Merlin held fast to each other. He placed Excalibur on the altar. He blessed Excalibur. Then gently picked her up. Galahad knelt down. Friar Thomas touched Galahad at the left shoulder then at the right with the point of Excalibur dubbing him King of Camelot. Then in a loud voice proclaimed: "RISE LORD GALAHAD, KING OF CAMELOT."

As Galahad rose to his feet Excalibur was placed in his trusting hands. Galahad kissed Excalibur then with the power of his office drew to Peter. Peter remained kneeling.

He then asked Peter: "Peter, are you here of your own free will?"

Peter answered: "I AM, MY LORD."

"Then I ask you: Will you, Peter my brother, take alliance with me as my First Knight?"

Peter answered: "I WILL SIRE."

Then His Lordship dubbed Peter first at the left shoulder then at the right shoulder, finishing with these words: "RISE SIR PETER, MY FIRST KNIGHT."

Peter rose to his feet. Both young men in a show of alliance crossed swords together before all of Camelot. The Heavens sang through Excalibur and Peter's swords. Arthur's boys were now his proud legacy. The people shouted: "LONG LIVE KING GALAHAD AND SIR PETER! LONG LIVE KING GALAHAD AND SIR PETER!"

While the crowd continued chanting, Galahad and Peter with the honor of their office drew to King Arthur. Both young men knelt before him. Honoring him with a sword salute. Galahad beckoned Sir Gawain, Sir William, Sir Frederick and Merlin to stand with them. Sir William held back hugging his son. Protocol came first. All six men saluted King Arthur, then hoisted Arthur's precious body onto the cremation bed.

The mass ended with a Sign of the Cross. Before the two priests and altar boys left the altar sight, Galahad had one wish-to see Peter and Sir William in front of him.

Father and son stood before their King. Galahad had both men hold each other at the forearms asking both men to take an oath. Both agreed to take the oath even though they knew not what that oath was. Galahad then said: "I ask you both to hold fast to each other. No matter what rank you hold in life, you are to remember that you are father and son."

Sir William knew why Galahad called for this oath. He answered: "I do Your Majesty," as did Peter follow his father's lead with the same answer of "I will Galahad, with all my heart." Sir William and Sir Peter then embraced each other and promised their King they would always remember this day forever.

Then the priest gave the men a blessing and left the altar.

"My Lord excuse me…Sire. There is a mass of people surrounding Galahad and Peter." Galahad finally answers Thomas.

"Good Father, what is it you wish?"

"When do we light the torch?"

"Later Father, when the people have all gone. I do not wish anyone hurt by the flames." Thomas nodded his head.

"Very good Your Majesty."

"Peter, where is Lady Arianna?" Peter sighted Arianna, for some reason she chose to be solitary at this most auspicious moment.

"My Lady, Galahad wishes a word with you."

"Sir Peter, you surprised us all. God blesses you."

Arianna hugged Peter then said: "You look wonderful. You and Galahad will make a good team together."

"Thank you My Lady."

Arianna kissed Peter on the cheek then said: "God go with you."

Then she drew to Galahad.

"My Lord."

"My Lady please, I am only Galahad to you." Arianna took Galahad's right hand, bowed her head and kissed his ring. Galahad was honored but also embarrassed.

"Excalibur looks well on you." Galahad drew her from her sheath. Arianna caressed her blade.

"How did you carry her? She is a heavy sword."

"Excalibur was my privilege and honor. There is never any weight in such an undertaking."

"I will learn these lessons." Both of Excalibur's guardians kissed her, then Galahad placed her in her sheath. Excalibur sang softly for them. Merlin and Nimue joined Galahad and Arianna. They stood side by side as though one family. The castle staff then paid their respects to their new King and his First Knight. After the pleasantries were taken care of, the people of Camelot were instructed to leave the square. Ralph, Percy, and John's bodies were removed from the altar sight, to be buried near Arthur's ashes tomorrow.

Lord Galahad turned to Sir Gawain and said: "Sir Gawain, tomorrow we must search for the other bodies, too many are lost."

"Sire we searched, some of them cannot be found. The others we will keep searching."

Sir William finally had the opportunity to speak with Peter.

"How on earth…?"

"Father, let me speak. Come by the steps, we will have some privacy there. Father an hour before mass, Galahad confronted me. The honor was so great that I could not turn away." Sir William places both hands on his sons' shoulders.

"You do realize my son that if something happens to Galahad you will become King."

"Father James apprised me of my position with Galahad. Galahad and I grew up as brothers, the least I can do is help him, and he in turn will be there for me."

"Your mother, God rest her, would be proud. As I am so very proud of you this day My Son."

Sir William and Sir Peter hugged each other with such great joy.

"Father, I have but one wish-that Galahad and I work a long, long time together for a common cause."

"HERE, HERE!"

Chapter Twenty-Five

THE FLAMES OF THE HOLY GHOST

Lord Galahad took rest on the verandah of the Round Table Room. It took almost all afternoon for Camelot to say good-bye to King Arthur. After a week of tragic affairs the bittersweet day had taken its toll. Galahad was quite fatigued. He asked for some buttermilk and sweetbread, a humble meal for a King.

Luke, a page in court, announced the square was now empty. It was now Galahad's heart-wrenching duty to order the Burning. Gazing out into the courtyard he said a silent prayer:

"Dear Father in Heaven
Help me send Uncle Arthur to you
Help me please take his place with dignity"

"Young Luke."
"My Lord. You called?"
"Please tell my men to assemble."
"And the others?"
"I will appease them." Luke bowed his head.
"Very good My Lord."

Galahad drew into the room, his heart pounding. He knew he had to choose one man to light the torch. He encircled the Round Table while all eyes befell on him. Sir Gawain, Sir William and Sir Frederick watched, waiting for Call to Orders. Galahad took Excalibur from her sheath and laid her at table. Sir Peter stood watch next to him. The men knew it was his call to seats. The women in the room huddled together quietly.

"I have assembled the men outside. I cannot ask one man to take on such a task as cremator, so I will not ask. I will act as cremator." Sir Gawain stood horrified.
"My Lord it is not your place."
"I know, but it is a horrible thing I have to ask. We all loved King Arthur."
A young man's voice replied: "I will act as Cremator."
"Luke, are you sure my son?"
Luke stood proud.
"That is, if you will help me father." Sir Gawain stood proud of his Luke.

Lord Galahad walked over to Luke, placed his arm around his shoulder and said: "You are a brave boy, young Luke. You will be my Squire at Court."

Sir Gawain and Lady Catherine were pleased. Gawain knew deep down that Luke would someday be a Knight of the Round Table as he is.

"Now both of you leave this room. We will follow hence."

Sir Gawain and Luke left the room. King Galahad retrieved Excalibur. Sir Peter and he beckoned all to follow. Arthur's mourners exited the castle. Just as when King Arthur's body was carried back to Camelot, a sword archway was made for Luke and Gawain to lead the procession. The torches were lit in hand. Father James and Friar Thomas blessed the fire.

"WE ASK THE HOLY GHOST TO TAKE OUR BELOVED KING ARTHUR TO HEAVEN."

The guards left their watch. Luke stood at the head, Gawain at the foot. The bell in the tower rang three times again.

Friar Thomas's voice followed the final peal.

"ARTHUR, KING OF CAMELOT WE COMMEND YOU TO GOD IN THE NAME OF THE FATHER AND OF THE SON AND OF THE HOLY GHOST. RECEIVE THE FLAMES OF THE HOLY GHOST."

The bell tower rang three more peals. At the third peal, Luke and Gawain lit the bed.

The sight was shocking yet humbling. Galahad held Peter at the shoulder and hence cried. Lady Catherine and Lady Arianna rushed to help them. The sight of the flames engulfing this man he loved was so overwhelming for this young King.

Realizing Galahad's grief, Gawain took charge ordering all back to the castle. The flames heat intensity became dangerous for all. Galahad refused to leave. He kept staring at King Arthur. It was as though he were paralyzed. Merlin dared to approach.

"My Lord please. King Arthur would not wish you harmed. Come watch the fire from the steps." Sir Peter stepped away.

Galahad paid one last tribute to King Arthur. He drew Excalibur from her sheath allowing the flames to touch her. EXCALIBUR sang for King Arthur one last time. Merlin then helped Galahad find the strength to leave.

Reaching the top step of the castle Galahad asked: "Merlin, please let me alone for a while." Merlin bowed his head to his King.

"I understand Sire."

From the doors Arianna and Merlin kept careful watch, holding onto each other, as though watching a son in pain. King Galahad with Excalibur watched the flames. Sir Peter joined his brother.

"Tomorrow when the flames are but a dream we will bury His Majesty King Arthur's ashes in AVALON."

Hence – "ARTHUR PENDRAGON, KING OF CAMELOT" will take his final resting-place in history.

Chapter Twenty-Six

CHECKMATE

"Mr. Lawrence, it seems I have won."

"I guess it's been longer than I thought." Jack ponders over his loss at chess.

"Perhaps you should practice more with Mrs. Lawrence."

"I agree Martin, my game was quite rusty."

"Dorothy, I see you have returned. Did all go well?"

"Mr. Lawrence, I have a message. The tour is running late. The expedition took in some extra sights." Jack is fidgeting with his Knights piece. He looks up at Dorothy.

"Extra sights?"

"It seems that they had a mock Viking funeral and not to worry, all is well."

Martin understood perfectly.

"Has the problem been taken care of?" Dorothy pours herself a glass of soda.

"Martin, all is in place. I will explain all to you later."

"Jack, care for another game?"

"Not right now. I guess I'll check on the kids."

Jack starts to make his way to the door then decides to ask: "Dorothy, do you know what time Arianna will be back?" It was already eight o'clock. Dorothy gazes down at her watch.

"I believe sometime this evening." Martin placed the game back in the wooden box.

"You know Martin, I did miss a great day, didn't I?"

"More than you know sir, more than you know." Jack left the room. Dorothy sat next to Martin with a gift of a rose from home.

"I have much to tell you."

Jack strolled back into the room asking: "Excuse me, but if there aren't any phone lines up there, how did you get a message?"

"Edmund sent one of our boys to the office. He left a note on my desk at the school."

"I see, well I think I'll join my son at the pool."

Both Dorothy and Martin took careful watch as Jack walked down the hall.

"What do you know? The chess game left off with Lady Arianna leaving to assist Merlin." Martin was rubbing his hands together anxiously waiting for an answer.

"Please tell me who is our new King." Dorothy held Martins' nervous hands in hers then answered.

"He is Galahad!" While bowing her head.

"Galahad, my word. He will be a good King."

"He most certainly will. One more surprise, Peter is his First Knight."

"Peter, my nephew?"

93

"Your nephew, Martin." They embraced with joy.

"This is good news."

"When I left, Lord Galahad and Sir Peter were standing at the steps watching King Arthur's cremation flames. Merlin asked that we meet Lady Arianna and he at the lake."

"What about Mr. Lawrence?"

"He has all the information he needs."

"Then we must hurry."

The Lady Nimue and Martin left the Dalton Hotel to assist the Lady Arianna to return home.

Chapter Twenty-Seven

GALAHAD'S PACT WITH ARIANNA

"My Lady."

"Merlin, my brother." Merlin smiled. He felt as though he finally had a sister, a sense of belonging.

"Nimue has gone already. We must plan your return."

"My return. Dear God, I have forgotten."

"I know you have, but the sky tells me we have but two, tops three hours to return." Now grief turns to fear.

"I cannot go back now, there is so much work to do." Merlin sees Arianna's despair. He also knows there will be no comforting it.

"Arianna please, you must return home. I cannot be responsible. You must go back to your life."

"Galahad will be so disappointed."

"I know, but his work is just beginning. In time, he will come to his own." Arianna knows her departure is inevitable. She asks Merlin.

"Please, can I have an hour before we tell them?" Arianna's eyes are so forlorning.

"I wish I could bring my family here." Merlin kisses Arianna on the hand, then holds both her hands to his heart.

He then says: " My dear sister, I would love nothing more, but they cannot survive here. Nobility is not in their hearts, as it is in yours." Merlin can feel Arianna's body start to tremble.

"Please, you must return and maybe in time they will receive nobility as a gift from you." Merlin is hoping Arianna can withstand the transition home.

"Come, let us join these good people for a small while. Then we must prepare." Arianna's heart sank even deeper. She could almost here the walls whisper "Please stay." Her chest hurt so badly-the pain, so intense, she cried bitterly. Merlin tried so hard to help her. She just buried her head in his chest and sobbed. Galahad heard her and came running to her aid.

"My Lady, what is wrong? Please I know we all grieve Uncle Arthur."

"Galahad, My Lord."

Merlin tries to explain: "Lady Arianna must take her leave before another day passes."

"Dear God, why? We just lost Uncle Arthur. I cannot lose Arianna also."

"My King, you do not realize that if she remains here Arianna's life will change drastically." Galahad's face shows nothing but dismay.

"Merlin, I do not understand."

"May we have a private moment in the Round Table Room?"

"By all means."

Catherine knew why Arianna was so upset. Trying to compose her she said: "Come Arianna, we will go to your room."

The two women presently climbed the stairs. Arthur's room, now Galahad's stood in their sights. Arianna dared open the door. Through the closed drapes the flames could be seen by the shadows they made. Arianna is despondently moving about.

"What is it my dear?"

"I cannot leave Catherine."

"What do you mean, you must!" Arianna's face is so downtrodden.

She angrily says, "Go home to what? A life of pain? A failing marriage? Problems that never seem to be resolved? Why? I could stay here and help Galahad."

Arianna did not know Merlin and Galahad were in the hall listening.

"At least I can help a young man who will hear what I have to say."

Galahad burst into the room yelling: "No, you must go!"

Arianna's eyes now have a crazed appearance about them.

"You heard me?"

"I did."

Arianna ran down the hall. Galahad ran after her, reaching for her.

"My Lady, I now know who you are."

Not meaning to show disrespect to her King, she says: "So what of it?" Galahad is trying to find words of comfort.

"Remember how you spoke of your son? You must return to him. Please, you must."

"Give me a reason why?"

"Someday he will be the man you wish him to be, but if you remain here he could very well end up becoming like Modred."

Arianna dropped to her knees sobbing. "I am so afraid to return home. Yet even more afraid of seeing my son grow as evil as Modred."

Galahad sat on the floor while he helped Arianna compose herself. Merlin looked down the hall; the whole castle staff took witness to this woman's strife and of their King's compassion.

Galahad held the shaking Arianna whispering softly: "Remember how you helped me promise that I will be the good man Uncle Arthur was?" Arianna was crying so.

"Sshh–Sshh. Remember-if I should have a son, I promised that I would raise him good and steadfast?"

"I remember."

"Rise with me." Galahad helped Arianna to her feet.

"Help her Merlin. Stay right there."

Galahad ran back to Uncle Arthur's room. In his hand were the two rings.

He said: "These rings mean nothing to Uncle Arthur any longer. If they can help you, then they serve a purpose."

Arianna stood there gazing, not quite comprehending.

"I need for you to promise me." Galahad drew Excalibur from her sheath. "Promise on Excalibur that you Lady Arianna will return to your family and teach them to stand proud as I stand proud with you this day."

Galahad held out Excalibur. Arianna stood there completely paralyzed. Merlin, Gawain and Catherine saw the turmoil on her face. Arianna had suffered so much, now her King is asking her to return to that loneliness. Could she?

Galahad's eyes and Arianna's eyes froze together. Arianna took strength from Galahad's eyes. She reached out and placed her hand on Excalibur. Tears engulfed her.

"I promise My Lord." Galahad returned Excalibur to her sheath.

"Now this will help you. Take Uncle Arthur's ring and wear it here." He placed it on Arianna's right hand forefinger. "I will wear this one here." Galahad placed the smaller silver ring on his right hand pinky finger.

"When all fails, hold the ring and take strength from it. Remember the promise and I will do the same."

"Thank You My Lord." Galahad is holding Arianna, comforting her.

"Lady Catherine."

"Sire."

"Please help Lady Arianna prepare."

Galahad placed a kiss on Arianna's ring then said: "I will escort you with Merlin to the lake."

The two women withdrew to Arianna's room. Galahad watched Arianna enter her room. He took hold of Excalibur's hilt, holding on for strength himself. EXCALIBUR SANG FOR HER KING.

Chapter Twenty-Eight

RETURN FROM CAMELOT

Arianna sat on the bed in her room gazing at this ring, weary from all her emotions. Catherine sat next to her. She lovingly said: "I will miss you."

"I know, and I will miss you."

A knock on the door interrupted them. Catherine moved to open the door.

"My Lady."

"Sir Peter?"

"Can I prepare you horse?"

"Sir Peter, Mark can take care of that now."

"Please Lady Catherine, I have been caring for Sir Brach all this time, he knows me."

"Then go. Arianna will be ready shortly." Sir Peter thusly kissed Arianna on the hand then left the room.

Catherine opened the wardrobe. She took Arianna's riding outfit out and laid it on the bed. Arianna looked at it then replied: "No wonder why you all thought me a man."

They both laughed bittersweetly. Arianna's stomach felt so tight, she could hardly get changed.

"I will help you." Arianna took off the beautiful black dress. She just stared at the outfit, then proceeded to dress herself. The slacks and the jacket felt confining. Catherine then helped Arianna with her boots. The silence was deafening but necessary. Catherine took the black dress and hung it. Arianna scanned the room. She closed her eyes to make a memory.

The ladies were about to leave the room when Arianna remembered her hat. As they drew from the room, the castle staff assembled in the halls and on the stairs. The array of people was breathtaking. In her riding outfit Arianna felt out of place, but the people who grew to love her made sure she was now a part of them. His Lordship Galahad's Knights were waiting in the Drawing Room. Catherine held fast as the doors opened. From the windows, dusk was now evident. King Arthur's flames were now embers. When Arianna walked into the Drawing Room the Knights lifted their swords.

Sir Gawain pounded the table with a hearty sounding "HERE, HERE!"

The Knights followed with: "LONG LIVE LADY ARIANNA, LONG LIVE LADY ARIANNA!"

Arianna could not believe the love this room was filled with. A love she felt very undeserving of.

"My Lady."

"Squire Luke."

"Lord Galahad is waiting with Merlin."

"Thank you."

While Arianna exited the room she could hear how much she would be missed. The Guards opened the castle doors. Galahad and Merlin were already on their horses. Sir Peter stood by with Sir Brach. Catherine and Arianna embraced.

"We will not say good-bye, no we will see each other again someday."
"When God wills it."
Arianna then took her leave. Sir Peter knelt before her and kissed her hand. Arianna kissed him on the cheek. Then said to him: "Help this young man."
Peter smiled. "Do not worry, I will."
Sir Peter helped Arianna mount her horse. Sir Gawain and Sir Frederick said their good-byes. Sir Brach snorted and Arianna patted him, giving the signal "Let us go!"
The three left the castle. As they rode through the Village Square the bell in the tower rang again and again. Friar Thomas met them at the gate then blessed Arianna's journey. The sound of the gates opening sounded cruel to Arianna. All she wished to do was shut them, hide behind them. Merlin suggested they take the southern route. It was getting dark and this way would be easier. Arianna noticed a burial taking place in the cemetery. Father James was performing the burial rights.
"Merlin, may I say good-bye?" Arianna pulled on the bridal.
"Father James?"
"My Dear child, I heard you were leaving."
"Who are you burying?"
"It is Modred, Arianna. King Arthur provided for his son."
A silent prayer was said and Arianna left. Father James cried out "Bless you my child."
On the way, the three spoke about the future. Arianna was mostly concerned about Alexis and her education. "Alexis is a good student, she will go far in her lifetime. She makes me so very proud of her."
"Arianna, you sound as Arthur did about Galahad." Merlin smiles at Arianna.
"Uncle Arthur was proud of me." Galahad sits tall in his saddle.
"He certainly was, Your Majesty."
"My Lady?"
"Galahad?"
"Do you know about the Holy Grail?"
"Indeed I do My Lord." Arianna's heart jumped for joy when Galahad asked the question.
"I would like to find it someday. Uncle Arthur tried and failed." Arianna and Galahad noticed the bittersweet memories on Merlin's face.
"It was unfortunate that His Lordship failed, but you will not my good King."
Galahad looks at Arianna with deep curiosity.
"Why do you say this?"
"I just have a feeling, that is all." Galahad gives Arianna a boyish smile.
"Then I will trust this feeling."
Arianna could tell they were near the water, the air suddenly got cooler. She stopped. It was not long enough for the scars of battle to have left this place. Arianna takes a deep cleansing breath.
"I am afraid we are here."

Galahad places his hand on his chest. He is astonished at the sights the battle has left behind. Galahad has never seen battle. Merlin rides ahead of them.

"Galahad, this is where His Majesty died."

The evidence stared them in the face as though they were in a nightmare. Pieces of armor, broken spears. Arrows lay all around. Some of Modred's men still lay unclaimed.

"MY GOD, HOW DID YOU FACE THIS?"

Arianna shrugged her shoulders, then said "We did, and unfortunately you will too someday."

Galahad replied "I pray this day will never come."

"Merlin, what will become of this?"

"Arianna, if no one claims them, we will retrieve the bodies and burn them."

"I see, Merlin."

Arianna looked around and with cynicism said "Nothing a good rain cannot clear up."

"Arianna, Galahad, I have a surprise for you."

"Merlin, is there time?

Merlin takes notice of the North Star, then tells Galahad "Galahad, hold Excalibur high. Point to the sky." Galahad obeyed.

"LADY OF THE LAKE, CAN YOU HEAR ME?"

"There really is a Lady of the Lake?" Merlin smiles.

"She exists, Galahad."

"Merlin, where is she?" Merlin searches the area.

"Since the battle, she must be in hiding."

"LADY OF THE LAKE, CAN YOU HEAR ME?"

"Hence from the Lake…"

"Merlin, she draws near."

Galahad becomes enchanted. He joyfully says: "Merlin, she is so beautiful."

"Merlin, Arianna, you have brought Lord Galahad to me." Galahad dismounts his horse. He walks over to The Lady as though he is hypnotized. The Lady's gentle voice tells him: "Come Forward Your Majesty."

"It is true. Excalibur did come from this lake." Her Ladyship smiles.

"She did My Lord." As Galahad knelt down to The Lady, he said these precious words: "I promise you this very day that I, Galahad, King of Camelot, will keep Excalibur close to my heart. I will use her honorably and remain steadfast to her precious powers."

"In God we trust."

Merlin and Arianna stood beside Galahad as though they were his proud parents. The beautiful Lady placed a kiss on Galahad's forehead.

"I know you will do us proud Galahad."

"Arianna, you will be taking your leave."

"Regrettably, My Lady."

"My Lady, is it possible that someday The Lady Arianna could return to Camelot?"

"Is this what you wish Lord Galahad?"

"I wish on Excalibur that before my life ends, The Lady Arianna returns to Camelot. Please."

Arianna was stunned at the request, for that matter so was Merlin.

"Arianna, do you wish the same?"

"Oh a thousand fold."

"Then look to the sky. Galahad raise Excalibur." He did.

"Draw an arch." Galahad obeyed the command. A beautiful rainbow appeared in the sky.

"Oh, My Lady." Then, a flock of geese appeared in the sky flying in the form of a sword; they flew under the rainbow.

"This is my call to Camelot. Whence you see this Arianna, prepare to return."

"How will I enter?"

"Hence the same way you came. An honor guard will wait for you."

Arianna bowed humbly to the Lady and with joy said, "Thank you so much. I can leave now. I am not afraid."

With these words Martin and Nimue appeared at the hilltop. The Lady and Arianna embraced, then she drew back to the lake. Arianna, Merlin and Galahad mounted their horses.

"Come, we will ride to the hill together." Arianna's stomach grew tight. Her back felt tense.

"Martin, how are you?" Martin got off his horse, showing respect, bowed to his King. Galahad humbly responded.

"Dear Martin. Please, you know me since I was a boy..."

"I am thankful and pleased that you are our King."

While Martin and Galahad spoke to each other, Merlin and Arianna told Nimue of the Lady's gift to Arianna and Galahad. Nimue responded joyfully, that she said "Oh Arianna, what a treasure."

"I am so happy that I can return."

"Indeed she can!" Galahad was so pleased that he ran over to Arianna and hugged her so hard. Arianna smiled finally. They were all so happy to see Arianna smile.

Arianna, thank you."

"Thank you? For what prey tell?"

Merlin takes both of Arianna's hands in his gentle hands cradling them to his chest. He tells her "After the tumultuous beginning we had, you remained steadfast."

"And I thank you for helping me realize my life has some special meaning. I am honored Excalibur chose me, she will remain in my heart forever."

"My Lady, the star, it shines brighter."

"Merlin, will you come with us?"

"Not now. I will escort Galahad home safely, and then I will meet with you later. All riders, mount their horses."

"Martin, excuse me, but do you not work at the Dalton?"

"For many years."

"Is all well with Jack and my children?"

"They are well My Lady, but Jack grows more anxious with your absence."

"A revelation. Maybe for once he will understand when he is absent."

Martin realizes the cynic in Arianna and rebuts her.

"He is a good man My Lady and he does love you." Arianna shakes her head.

"I know, Martin."

Arianna looked around. Her world lay on the other side of the hill.

"Merlin, one minute please." She dismounted Sir Brach.

"Please, My Lord Galahad…"

"Please Arianna, do not even say the words."

"I dare not. I will hold fast to our promise."

"I have but one request." Arianna's expression is questionable.

"My Lord?"

"When you return, please bring Joseph."

Arianna smiled. "I will My Lord." Then she knelt to her King.

Upon rising she said, "Now I have but one request." Galahad's expression is now questionable.

"I will return, but until then keep a picture of me in your heart."

Arianna put her hand on Galahad's heart. Galahad kissed her hand and then embraced her with all the love his heart could give.

The Lady Arianna escorted by Nimue and Martin exited Camelot, riding over the hill. Galahad drew Excalibur from her sheath. She sang her song of farewell to her guardian.

There was a full moon when they reached the other side. Arianna took notice of the lake with that ridiculous fountain.

"That sign Nimue, "Merlin's Pond.""

"What of it, My Lady?"

"Martin, people should only know the truth."

"The problem is, if people really knew the truth, they could not possibly understand."

"You are most correct Martin."

"Now how do I explain things to Jack?" The horses pick up the pace on their cantor.

"Not to worry, we have an idea, but first you should know that Jack knows the tour ran late. We gave him the message in the game room."

Arianna thought to herself "Message, game room, I wonder?"

"Martin, you have no idea how Jack can be."

"I guess we will find out, will we not?"

"Martin, I know you work at the Dalton, are you related to Sir Gawain or Catherine?"

"I am Sir Peter's Uncle. I am William's brother and I too am a Knight of the Round Table."

"Then you are Sir Martin. It is my honor to be in your calibrated company My Lord." Martin's face showed the pride he carried for his office.

"My Lady, I must say, the minute I met you I had a feeling you were the one Excalibur would choose." Arianna bowed her head humbly.

"Nimue when I leave, will you both return to Camelot?"

"We shall, the Riding Academy will be a place for people to rent a horse and enjoy the countryside."

Then the Lady Nimue auspiciously said:

"THE HILL TO CAMELOT IS ONLY FOR THOSE WHO BELIEVE!"

Chapter Twenty-Nine

THE DALTON

The horses were returned to the Riding Academy. Lady Arianna brought Sir Brach in personally.

"Thank you Sir Brach for all your help." Arianna then gave him a handful of sugar cubes and a kiss on the snout. She left in haste.

As Nimue, Martin and Arianna got in the car, Arianna assessed "Cars, what a waste."

"We agree."

"I am so scared," Arianna said as they rode down the causeway.

"I do not understand Arianna, you stood on battleground, you witnessed Arthur's death, how can you be afraid now?"

"I have never lied to Jack about anything except for his thirtieth surprise birthday party. I really do not know how to explain all this."

Arianna catches her reflection in the car window. "Look at me, I am in a riding costume, we are in riding costumes. I will just say we were running late and did not have time to change." Arianna ganders at Martin's watch.

"Well it is ten thirty, then it is the truth. We are late."

"My Lady…"

"Please Sir Martin, you must stop calling me this."

Martin smiled. "I know, the title just suits you."

"Arianna, we have a plan to make things up to Jack. We are planning to invite all of you on a tour to the Museum of Kings."

"Nimue, how will that help?"

"It will look as though the hotel is taking blame and it lets you off the hook."

"What is the Museum of Kings?"

"It was an old mansion owned by a man named Atherton. He was very rich and loved royalty. When he died he left the mansion to Parliament. They in turn made it "The Museum of Kings."

"Does any one else know about me?"

"One more person-my nephew Charles, the Guest Director. He will make sure all is taken care of when you depart for New York."

Their car reached the city. London is beautiful at night. Charles was already waiting for them at the main door.

"My Lady."

"Mr. Charles, what time is it?"

"It is eleven thirty. The children are asleep. Mrs. Andrews is with them. Mr. Lawrence is in the lounge."

"Is he very upset?" Arianna nervously played with her hat.

"If he is, he is not showing it very much, except for that funny twitch in his face." Arianna put her hand on her stomach, then took a deep breath and walked in the door. Arianna stood in the lobby. The area was quiet. She put her hands behind her back, trying to think, but it was to no avail.

She said, "Damn these bloody lights. I know he is upset."

Arianna paced the lounge floor. She kept pacing and staring at the lounge door not knowing how to face Jack. Merlin strolled in, realizing that something was gravely wrong. Nimue noticed him standing by the sofa watching the situation at hand.

"What are you doing here?"

"Something told me to return. My Love, what is going on?"

"I do not know, Merlin." Arianna had no idea Merlin was standing there.

"Is Galahad safe?"

"His Lordship is home, all is well." Arianna's nerves have taken control of her. This is not good. "Nimue, this woman can weather a storm. You should have seen her. She stood in front of me at the lake. I almost killed her with Excalibur! She never even blinked an eye, her mind was fixed on her mission. Yet before we left, she was terrified to come home. Now I know why. Look at her, she is frozen."

"Go help her." Merlin tapped Arianna on the shoulder. Arianna became startled.

"Arianna please, no disrespect intended, but what evil spell does this man have on you?" Arianna is now turning Galahad's ring around her finger.

"I don't know Merlin, he makes me fell inadequate. Let me explain, from the beginning Jack did not wish to travel here. Now I take all this time away and I feel guilty."

"Guilty for what? My dear please, there is no guilt when you follow your heart, as long as it is a pure one." Nimue comes to Arianna's aid. She takes hold of her hand.

"My sister, when I spent so much time away with Arthur, Nimue never made me feel guilty. She knew my cause, my work was important."

Merlin takes Arianna by the forearm. He says "Come, we will go together." Jack heard Arianna's voice. Angrily, he drew out of the lounge.

"What the hell happened?" Arianna cringes at the sound of Jack's voice.

"Mr. Lawrence, I am Edmund Winters…"

"Jack, I am sorry, but the tour ran late. We were having a beautiful time. Did you at least have a good day?"

"The kids drove me crazy as usual. I could have stayed home for a day like this." Merlin interrupts. He is trying to help.

"Mr. Lawrence…"

Jack points to Merlin asking, "Who is he?"

"I am Mrs. Lawrence's tour guide." Arianna nervously cuts off Merlin.

"Jack, didn't you do anything with the children?" Jack reacts to Arianna's question with such sarcasm.

"Yes, thanks to Martin. He made arrangements for the kids, and Martin and I played a long game of chess."

"Well, at least you all had some fun. It was not a boring day."

Arianna then realizes Jack and Sir Martin were both playing the chess game.

105

"Mr. Lawrence, we realize you were inconvenienced."

"That's for sure!" Dorothy hears the animosity in Jack's voice. The sound intimidates Arianna. Arianna has that I am guilty look about her. She decides to approach Jack with caution.

"Mr. Lawrence, we would like for you and your children to join us at the "Museum of Kings" tomorrow."

"Museum of Kings, what is that?"

"It is a half mile from where our tour was and we could all go horseback riding up to the museum." Jack folds his arms in front of him. It is his way of closing the door on the world.

"I guess that will be nice." Merlin tries to break the tension.

"Good, then it is all arranged."

Jack takes a bamboozled glance at his wife and asks: "Ari, where are your clothes?"

Arianna grabs hold of her jacket lapels and tries to explain.

"Jack, there was no time to change, so when we go tomorrow I will get my clothes." Arianna then takes a deep breath and bravely says "Jack, I hate to say this but you could have joined me. You chose to stay behind."

Jack then takes his defensive stance by placing both his hands on his hips and rebuts with "The whole idea did not interest me."

Arianna throws her hat up in the air, almost hitting the chandelier and rebuts Jack with "Exactly Jack! Please, I am tired and I wish to go to bed." Merlin and Nimue knew Arianna would be all right. Her persona seems positive. They kiss her good night and walk away.

"We will see you in the morning." Arianna throws a kiss.

As they walk away, Nimue and Merlin hear Jack commenting to Arianna: "You know Ari, you look different in that suit."

Arianna raises her eyebrows at the comment and asks "Different, how different?"

"I don't know. I can't describe it, but it's as though you are someone else."

Arianna gave a slight cough.

"Merlin, Jack should only know that his wife is royalty."

Merlin shakes his head in agreement and replies "I know Martin, I know."

There was a strange quiet with Arianna. She was quite withdrawn this evening. When they retired to their rooms, Arianna dismissed Mrs. Andrews, then presently checked on the children. She kissed Alexis, then Joseph. Leaning over Joseph, gazing at this boy, who seemed so angelic in his sleep, made her wonder about how Modred must have been when he was a boy. The two of them were so alike. Arianna said a prayer to herself asking God to help her change Joseph before it was too late.

While putting on her nightgown Jack became concerned asking "Are you alright?"

"I am My L... Yes Jack."

"You are so quiet." Arianna started brushing her hair.

"I am fine. I am just tired."

Arianna and Jack kissed each other good night. Jack fell sound asleep but Arianna remained wide awake. She pulled a chair to the window. The view was of the city of London, beautifully lit, just like Manhattan. Sitting there, her mind could not forget the flames and Galahad's face when the flames took over Arthur's body. How humbling this all was to him, to all of them. How did God allow her to witness this? What was his plan for her? She watched Jack sleep. Her tired mind finally allowed Arianna to mourn Arthur. She buried her face in a pillow and cried, crying herself to sleep in the chair.

Arianna woke up around six A.M. with her back bothering her from sleeping in a chair all night. She then put herself in bed, her mind wondering as to what could possibly be in the "Museum of Kings."

It was now seven A.M. Alexis woke up to find mom awake in bed.

"Mom, what time did you come home?"

"Very late honey?"

Arianna decided it was to no avail to go back to sleep. Nimue and Merlin would be here later, time to get up and shower. A bathroom, what a treasure. This morning, breakfast was served in the main dining room. The morning routine felt like a state of chaos even though Arianna and her family sat down to a breakfast fit for a queen.

"Excuse me My Lady, but is your breakfast to your liking?" Arianna looked up from her coffee cup. It was Charles.

Arianna smiled and said "Very much thank you." Then fidgeted with her napkin. Jack looked so very baffled. He kept scratching the back of his head.

"I will have a car waiting for you at eleven o'clock."

"That will be fine."

"Good Morning Arianna."

"Good Morning Mer...Edmund."

"Did you rest well?"

"As well as can be expected."

Edmund took Arianna's hand and gently kissed it, making Jack feel jealous for some reason.

"Mr. Lawrence, are you a horseman?"

"I am not, Mr. Winters."

"Too bad. Your wife is a wonderful horsewoman." Jack's face was red.

"Alexis, Joseph. Dorothy is wondering if you would care to go riding with us later?" Their eyes jumped out of their sockets.

"Where?"

"Yeah where?"

"To the museum." Alexis and Joseph were out of their seats begging.

"Could we mom, please?" Arianna sat back throwing her napkin on the table.

"Now you both want to go. Amazing."

"Please, Please." Arianna snickered.

"I guess we can." Arianna could not understand how both children had such a change of heart. They were unreasonably excited.

"Thank you mom. Thank you."

"Edmund, where is Dorothy?"

"She is in Martin's office." Arianna looked like a little girl in a candy shop.

"Oh wonderful. I will be right back."

While leaving the table mom heard Alexis ask Edmund "Don't you people call Ladies "My Lady" only when they are royalty?" Arianna stopped short to hear Merlin's answer.

"Why yes my child, most of the time." Alexis' curiosity is now charged.

"Then why my Mom?" Merlin smiled charmingly.

"Your mother is royalty my dear." Alexis tapped her fingernails on the table trying to understand.

She said "Huh I – what?"

Merlin took a laissez-faire stance to the situation. Then rebutted with "My dear child do not try to understand."

"Daddy." Jack was too preoccupied with Arianna just leaving the table as she did. He did not hear Alexis.

"Dad!"

"What is it Alexis?"

"What the heck is going on with mom?"

"I would like to know myself."

"Royalty, you've got to be kidding. Mom's just mom from Glendale, Queens, New York."

"Kids, I think all that forest air went to their brains. I've never seen your mother act like this. Something's up."

Arianna and Dorothy came walking back to the table. Arianna spied Jack still sitting there.

"Well Jack, are you going to stay here all day or are you going to come and enjoy a piece of heaven?" Jack stood from the table.

"Do I have to wear a riding outfit?"

"Not if you do not wish to Mr. Lawrence."

Jack defensively put his hands in his pockets and replied "Then I'll come."

"It is ten-thirty. Let's all get ready."

Arianna was so eager to get going. She had all her gear ready.

Chapter Thirty

THE MUSEUM OF KINGS

It took an hour to drive up to the riding school. Alexis was in total awe of her surroundings. She quaintly said to Martin "No wonder why my mom loves it here."

"You have a keen eye young lady. The landscape is quite beautiful."

"Come Alexis, we will get into our riding attire."

Jack and Joseph chose to play ball while the girls got ready.

"Jack, you are totally detached from all this." He and Joseph kept playing catch.

Jack answered "Dorothy, stuff like this just doesn't impress me."

"May I ask why?"

Jack shrugged his shoulders.

"No reason. It just doesn't." Dorothy fastened her bootstrap, sneering at Jack.

"I see."

They all heard Alexis come out of the changing room laughing. Jack turned to see what the commotion was all about.

"So Dad, how do I look?"

To Jack, Alexis looked weird in the outfit. He answered "You look cute honey."

"I feel dorky."

"Where's your mother?"

Alexis pointed eastward. "She went to the stables."

Edmund now comes from the office in full attire.

"Mr. Lawrence, I think your wife to be born in the wrong century." Jack now looked curious at Edmund for the statement he just heard.

"What do you mean Mr. Winters?"

"Have you looked at her lately?"

"Mr. Winter's, its this country or that dumb outfit."

Edmund squints at Jack, with contempt he rebuts "Arianna is an old fashioned woman. She should be respected as such."

"Hey Dad look at the deer over there. There's got to be at least a hundred of them." Martin appears now completely ready.

"At least young Joseph, deer live here all year long. When they learn to trust you they come right to the fence and we feed them."

Sir Brach was so happy to see Arianna. He caressed her face with his gentle snout.

"I missed you too." The stable boy had him ready in gear for her.

"Arianna, here you are."

"Merlin, here is where I belong."

"We now understand my dear, remember the promise."

"It is amazing how he has not questioned about Arthur's ring."

"He will not. I know this kind of man." Merlin takes a handful of oats to feed Sir Brach.

"Arianna please, before they get suspicious. We will take route "B" to the lake."

"OK."

"I must speak with you about a matter of urgency." Arianna gazed deeply into Merlin's hypnotic eyes.

"What is it dear friend?"

"When we get there, please mount Sir Brach."

To Jack and the children's surprise, Merlin and Arianna rode out of the stables with Arianna on Brach.

"Mom, you look like Princess Diana." Arianna smiled with pride.

"Thank you Alexis." Arianna could see that Jack agreed, but he did not say anything. The stable boy led their horses out.

"Arianna, are you ready to go?" Arianna held fast on the bridal.

"In a heartbeat Dorothy."

"Well, mount up everyone."

The riding party rode out. Nimue took Jack, Joseph and Alexis on route "A". Merlin and Arianna on route "B".

"Mr. Winters why are you and Mom going that way?"

"Your mother is an experienced rider young man."

As they rode ahead they could see Dorothy's riding party slowly making their way. Merlin and Arianna rode past the lake. Arianna went on to check if the hole where she drew Excalibur from was still there.

"It is still there My Lady." Arianna shivered. What she thought to be a fantasy was really truth. Arianna dismounted her horse. She walked over to where King Arthur and Modred died. Arianna caressed the grass where his body lay.

Merlin looked around saying "My Lady Arianna there is something I must tell you." Arianna became concerned with the seriousness in Merlin's voice.

"What dear friend?" Merlin placed his hand over his mouth trying to find the words to tell her. He sighs.

"Galahad and you changed both of your histories."

"How?"

"With a promise to return and something you told him before you left."

"I do not understand."

"Remember that you told Galahad to keep a picture of you in his heart?"

Arianna folded her arms and said, "All right, go on."

"Not only did he keep a picture of you in his heart, he painted you."

Arianna was astonished. She placed her hand over her heart.

"Are you telling me that I am in the Museum of Kings?"

"You are, my sister."

"Dear God, Jack must be told."

"Listen to me, they will not fully comprehend what they are seeing. Somehow Jack might only see a pretense of you."

Arianna takes a deep cleansing breath and says, "Let us hope."

Dorothy's riding party caught up. Joseph became so exited when he saw the lake.

"Mommy, mommy do you see over there, there's a wishing pond. Could we get off and make a wish?"

"Mr. Winters it is beautiful." Edmund smiled.

"It is Mr. Lawrence."

"Mrs. Winters, was there really a Lady of the Lake?"

Jack picked up a rock throwing it in the lake. He tells Joseph "Only in story books Joseph."

Arianna standing there somewhat miffed states "I beg to differ with you Jack."

"Ari you can't believe in this."

Hearing contempt in Jack's voice, Arianna answers "Oh but Jack I do, with all my heart."

Sir Brach caressed Arianna on the face then he snorted. Arianna whispered to him, " You understand me my faithful steed."

"Daddy could we make a wish?" Alexis read the poem:

SEE
THE LADY OF THE LAKE
THROW A PENCE AND
MAKE HER WAKE
MAKE A WISH
WISH IT WELL
MAYBE MERLIN
WILL CAST A SPELL

Jack gave both the children a coin to throw. Alexis and Joseph closed their eyes, making a wish and then threw the coin.

Alexis turned around and said "Hey Mom, wouldn't it be funny if Merlin showed up and really cast a spell?"

Arianna, Merlin and Nimue laughed together. Jack looked strangely at them.

"Oh sure Alexis, maybe Merlin or maybe King Arthur is right over the hill."

Merlin noticed Arianna took Brach back to where Arthur died just two days ago. Her face was blanched with mourning. Merlin respected her privacy.

"Oh Dad, King Arthur isn't there."

"One never knows does one, Mr. Lawrence." Jack shrugged his shoulders.

"Shall we continue?"

"Mrs. Winters, why can't we just take a car to the museum?"

"If we go by car Alexis we will miss all this beautiful scenery."

"Mr. Winters, can we go to the ruins of Camelot?" Merlin stopped dead in his tracks quickly reaching for an answer.

"Mr. Lawrence, the tour for Camelot is closed today."

"Oh, too bad."

"Is everyone here? Let us cross the hill."

Arianna took pause with Sir Brach. Chills ran through her. Here she will be allowed entrance to Camelot. In her heart Arianna wished she could take Sir Brach and run away, rip through the forest and never return.

"Mom, come on!" Arianna sighed.

"Coming Joseph."

"Dorothy, come ride next to me. Please tell me what is the real answer, where is the road?"

"The museum will be opened to the public as of tomorrow. Today is reserved for you My Lady. You are to be our first guest."

Arianna sat tall in her saddle, but smiled bittersweetly.

"I am honored."

The Mansion was straight ahead. It was a beautiful structure, made of tan and brown bricks. Tan towers on the roof, both with portholes adorning it and arch framed windows. The mansion carried fourteen rooms and was surrounded by a beautiful green lawn, tall handsome trees and all species of roses and flowers. A shear delight for the eye.

They all dismounted. All the horses were tied to the rails near the landing. Merlin walked quickly ahead.

A woman came to the door asking "Is her Ladyship really here?"

Merlin smiled in his boyish way saying "Cynthia, she is but seconds into the door."

"Arianna may I see you please?" Merlin heard excited anticipation from inside the museum. Arianna ran ahead quickly.

"Take my arm." Merlin escorted The Lady Arianna into the main door. Excalibur's Guardian took her place in history and as first guest of honor.

"Dad why did Mr. Winters do that with Mom?"

"I don't know Alexis, I guess it is all part of the tour. Let's just have fun."

Jack and the children followed.

"This place is interesting."

Merlin turned to Jack. "Interesting Mr. Lawrence? That's just the half of it."

"Dad how long is this gonna take?"

"Relax Joseph, look around. Maybe you will finally learn something."

All the rooms were dedicated to the Kings and their Knights. There were three Kings here: King Arthur, King Galahad and King Henry the First. Each room bedecked with the clothes and the jewels they wore. The other room was dedicated to the great Armor used. Also a room dedicated to the horses and their armor. Joseph's mouth was wide open to the size of the horses.

"Mom that horse looks so real I wish I could ride him."

"He does look real Joseph."

Cynthia opened a door to what was "The Round Table Room". Atherton had the exact room rebuilt in The Museum. When Arianna drew into the room the museum staff all beheld her. Jack and the children looked around. Arianna moved straight toward Arthur's chair. Merlin watched as she held on as she tried to swallow tears but they would not hold. Under her breath she whispered "Arthur I love you, sleep well. I hope you found peace."

"Arianna are you all right?"

"It is the ambiance Jack. It is so beautiful. Please, I would like to go to "King Arthur's Room." They climbed the stairs.

"Mom can we go home?"

"Later Joseph." As usual Joseph had to put a damper on the mood of the moment.

"Mom I'm bored. I want to go home!" Arianna tried to remain patient.

"I said later Joseph." Arianna now walked into Arthur's room.

The whole room was eager as to Arianna's response. Cynthia said "Welcome, My Lady."

A painting of King Arthur hung on the center wall. Under it was EXCALIBUR a befitting tribute to her revered owner. Arianna's eyes filled with tears. She rubbed her hand over the case. Arianna quietly says "Hello old friend."

"So that's what he looked like. He was very dignified."

"He was at that Mr. Lawrence."

"My Lady, would you like to hold her?" Arianna's face said it all. The case was unlocked. Merlin drew Excalibur from her case. As he gave Excalibur to The Lady Arianna, she sang. Arianna kissed her. Excalibur was safe again in her guardians trusting hands. Jack and the children could not comprehend what they were witnessing.

Jack shrugged his shoulders as usual then responded "Let's keep going, we know Mom could stay here all day."

"Yeah she loves this stuff."

Jack decided to do some exploring by himself. There were so many artifacts. Alexis decided to stay by Mom.

"Mom, is this really Excalibur?" Arianna's smile radiated the room as she answered the question.

"Alexis, this is truly Excalibur."

"She is so beautiful. May I hold her?" Arianna glanced at Merlin for direction.

Merlin said "Young lady you can touch her but you cannot hold her."

Alexis touched her hilt and then caressed her blade.

"She is so smooth and shiny."

"I see young lady that you have respect for the finer things in life."

"Sometimes Mrs. Winters."

Now Jack ganders back in the room, his wife and daughter were so enthused by that sword. He wondered why. Here he stood by a painting, whispering to himself "Here is a beautiful woman."

This woman he admired had long brown flowing hair over one shoulder, wearing a beautiful red rose and gold dress. Her hands were crossed in her lap. On her forefinger she wore a silver ring. There under the painting sat a plaque it read:

THE LADY ARIANNA LAWRENCE
"EXCALIBUR'S FOUNDING GUARDIAN"

Entranced at this picture, Jack realized that the woman for some reason resembled Arianna. His eyes waved back and forth to confirm this. He also assessed that the woman and Arianna had the same name. A light went off at the end of the tunnel. Jack thought to himself "No wonder these people treat my wife as royalty, she looks so much like this here lady and they both have the same name. Dear God, they think she is her ancestor!"

Jack confirms his thoughts with a shake of the head and a rub on the chin. Then says, "So that's it!"

"Joseph come here."

"When are we leaving?" Joseph started making his animal noises.

"Go get mom, Joseph."

"WHY?" Joseph's body is shaking traumatically.

"Enough Joseph! Go get your mother. I would like her to see this picture."

"But Dad…"

"Go now Joseph!"

Angrily Joseph made his way to his mother.

"Mom, when are we leaving?"

Merlin's face takes on an annoying expression at Joseph's behavior. He tells Joseph with sternness "When the tour is over young man." Joseph's oppositional tendencies are showing themselves gravely.

"MOM! WHEN ARE WE LEAVING?" Arianna decided not to answer.

"MOM!" Merlin tries to pull Joseph away.

"Young man, when your mother is finished here we will all leave."

"Hey I want to touch that thingy thing too!"

Joseph reached out so fast Merlin could not stop him. When Joseph's hand touched Excalibur, Joseph received a jolt.

"OWW! THAT HURTS!" His hand was thought to have been burned.

Jack pulled on Joseph screaming "What the hell is that?"

The whole room went crazy. Cynthia cried out "How disrespectful!"

"What the heck is that Ari?" Arianna is now so embarrassed by her son's behavior that she goes deeply on the defensive.

"Jack, he deserved that!" Dorothy checked Joseph's hand as Merlin tried to explain.

"The hand does not appear to be burned," but Cynthia gets some ice just for precaution."

"Mr. Lawrence, please understand that according to legend, Excalibur can only be handled by a good man or woman with only the best intentions to use her. Excalibur was only at her defense."

"Please Mr. Winters, this is all a hoax to me."

"Excuse me, both of you. Jack please…"

"Don't Jack me Arianna, you care more for this sword than your own son! Arianna now protected Excalibur almost bodily.

"What kind of jerk do you think I am? Come Arianna we are leaving!"

Jack grabbed for his wife's hand and received a similar response.

He held tight on his hand, yelling, "This is insane!"

"I am not leaving Jack!"

Merlin turned to Nimue saying to his wife "I know now why she feared returning."

Martin and Charles appeared from the back room concerned about Arianna.

"Are you alright My Lady?"

"I am thank you. Please put Excalibur back in her case."

Arianna gently kissed Excalibur at the pommel then handed her to Martin. Jack was completely dumbfounded.

"What? Why doesn't it hurt you?"

"Dad…"

"Not now Alexis."

"Dad come here." Jack went next to Alexis.

"Look down!"

In the display case was a cross and chain. Under the cross read

FAVOR GIVEN TO KING ARTHUR
BY THE LADY ARIANNA LAWRENCE
BEFORE FATAL BATTLE WITH MODRED

"Mom, why does this look so much like your cross?"

"Are you wearing your cross?"

Arianna put her hand on her chest and answered her daughter. "I am not wearing my cross." Arianna viewed the cross on display. Jack and Alexis watched this mystery unfold.

Arianna looked at her cross then she angrily eyes Merlin asking, "Why was this not burned with Arthur?" Jack twitched his eyebrows.

"You can't mean King Arthur?"

"Indeed I do Jack." Arianna looked into Jack's unbelieving eyes and broke down. Jack just stood there.

"Daddy, is mommy ok?"

"I think so Joseph. How's your hand?" Joseph played with his hand.

"Oh, it is fine."

"My Lady would you like to hold your cross?"

"Please Cynthia." Cynthia opened the case and then gave the cross to Arianna. The cross had aged, even though to Arianna, Arthur died just two days ago.

"What is this nick in the gold, Cynthia?"

"It is Modred's blade mark. When it was removed from King Arthur it was there." Cynthia knew that what she was about to say would hurt Arianna deeply.

She takes Arianna's hands and says "My Lady Arianna, what now appears to be dirt is His Majesty's blood stain."

The cross fell to the floor.

"This is a joke."

"Mr. Lawrence, I assure you it is not a joke." Jack then points to the painting.

"Then I guess this stupid painting is my wife also."

Merlin eyes the beautiful painting then proudly says, "You could say that."

Jack sneers at Merlin in contempt and says "Oh come now!"

Arianna rubbed the nick on the cross. Her voice became ever so melancholy.

"When Arthur's breastplate broke, this was the fatal stroke." Merlin came to Arianna's aid. He stood in back of her and placed both hands on her shaky shoulders.

"Martin, get Her Ladyship a glass of wine." Martin left the room.

"My Lady would you…" Arianna shaking her head she already knew the question.

"Cynthia keep it here with all the rest. I gave the cross to King Arthur. I have no claim to it." Martin handed Arianna a glass of zinfandel.

Cynthia gently put the cross back in the case. Jack stood there scratching his head trying hard to digest all of this. Alexis came to her father's aid.

"Dad please listen to me. While I was in the library I borrowed a book. This whole unbelievable story is in the book Dad." Jack is now tapping his nails on the case.

"I don't understand it either, but listen. The book tells about how a woman finds Excalibur buried in the soil and somehow ends up back in Camelot to help Merlin and Arthur. After Arthur dies she gives Excalibur to Galahad."

Alexis turned around and inquisitively asks "Mr. Winters, could you possibly be Merlin?" Merlin folded his arms and snickered.

"Alexis, you are an astute young lady. Would you care for a brandy Mr. Lawrence?" Dorothy came out with a snifter.

While placing the snifter in Jack's hand, Alexis eyed her saying "Mrs. Winters if your husband is Merlin than you must be Lady Nimue."

Nimue responded the same way that her husband did. She said "You are astute my child."

Merlin thereafter went over to Alexis and kissed her on the forehead. Then he drew to Jack trying to explain everything to him.

"Listen Mr. Winters or Merlin or whomever you are. I hear this, I see this but I really don't think I understand or believe it." Jack laughs nervously. "To me it's a hoax and I do not understand why my wife is part of it."

Arianna, moved by Excalibur removing her from her case that with the courage of her convictions met Jack's eyes as they were frozen together. Arianna then placed Excalibur's point to the floor and held on to the hilt, leaning on it with both hands as though a cane. Jack eyed his wife's stance. She looked like a Knight in waiting battle mode.

He then shrugged it off by saying "Joseph, Alexis, if your mother wishes to stay she can. I am leaving!"

Arianna watched Jack leave. Her face filled with despair, she held onto Excalibur's hilt and twirled Galahad's ring repeating to herself "Remember the promise, remember the promise."

Alexis ran into the hall calling her father back. She said "DAD IF YOU HAVE TROUBLE UNDERSTANDING THIS THEN THERE IS NO MAGIC IN

YOUR HEART OR ANYWHERE. DAD IF YOU BELIEVE IN THE MAGIC, THE MAGIC WILL BELIEVE IN YOU."

At that moment Excalibur sang in Arianna's hand. Arianna smiled with contentment. Alexis believed whole-heartedly that her mother was so special.

Jack still believed it a hoax and left with Joseph.

Arianna hugged Alexis and said to her daughter, stroking her cheek "Thank you my child."

Deciding not to feel guilty and leave she turned to Cynthia and asked, "Cynthia, is there a portrait of Galahad?"

"This way My Lady." Cynthia escorted The Lady Arianna and her daughter Alexis to Galahad's room. There a portrait of Galahad holding Excalibur and in the foreground a picture of the Holy Grail.

The staff saw the pride on Arianna's face as she happily said, "I knew he would find it."

"Find what Mom?" Arianna was so entranced by the picture.

"The Holy Grail...Huh? I will tell you about it another time."

"Mom, not for anything but Galahad looks like an older version of Leonardo DiCaprio." Arianna laughed at the statement.

"He does doesn't he."

Alexis spied the ring on Mom's hand asking "Mom, what is that silver ring on your hand?"

"It is a gift from His Lordship, Galahad." In the picture Galahad was wearing his ring. Alexis took her mother's hand in hers gazing at the ring.

"Mom, it is beautiful."

"My Lady, in the confusion I did not formally introduce myself. I am Cynthia Wells, Galahad's great-great Granddaughter."

"Oh my dear girl." Arianna and Cynthia hugged each other for joy.

"Please, can I see my painting?"

"Come, please." Cynthia presented Arianna and Alexis the beautiful portrait.

"Look Mom, you are wearing your ring also."

Arianna was honored by how Galahad painted her. She glanced at the ring in the portrait and the one on her hand. Merlin and Nimue joined them. Merlin held Arianna's hand and tenderly kissed it. She held the promise in her heart and knew that someday when Galahad needed her, she would return. She then walked back to King Arthur's room. The Lady Arianna Lawrence then kissed Excalibur and gently placed her in her precious casing for all time.

EPILOGUE

THE AIRPORT

Merlin and Lady Nimue escorted Lady Arianna and her family to the airport with Charles as their chauffeur. Saying good-bye was now a hard task. Merlin reminded Arianna that they would see each other again. Jack and Joseph were still perplexed about it all. Nimue hugged and kissed the children and shook Jack's hand. Nimue hugged and kissed Arianna. They could hardly let go. Charles followed but more discreetly. Merlin did the same.

When he came to Arianna he kissed her hand and then embraced her, whispering sweetly in her ear "Remember My Lady, look to the sky and always follow your heart." Arianna was shaking.

Merlin drew a small box from his pocket. Arianna wondered what it could be.

"Arianna, please take this with you. Do not open it until you are on the plane."

Arianna placed the small box in her purse. Then with courage both Merlin and Arianna embraced again and said a painstaking and tearful "Farewell for now."

Upon taking their seats, Arianna anxiously opened the box. Seeing the contents of the box brought tears to her soul. It was her cross. With it a note:

Dearest Arianna,

This cross you gave to Arthur to wear for protection. Wear it in memory of His Majesty and feel Christ shield you from harm. Our King Arthur will always be with you, as will I. He wishes this for you dearest sister. For the Love of Camelot.

With all our love,
Merlin and Nimue
'DEUS LE VOLT'
(God wills it)

Arianna put the cross on, looked out her window and whispered "I will look to the sky, Arthur."

The Lawrence family returned to New York. Jack was told the whole story and still could not comprehend it.

That week, it was time for Joseph's meeting with his social worker at the Tourette's Foundation and for Jack's home care therapy.

While taking his treatment Jack decided to go through and label their vacation tapes. He put a tape in the VCR. Arianna had forgotten about one part of her trip. As she was preparing lunch for her family she heard from the television in the living room "DEAR GOD YOUR EXCALIBUR!" Her legs weakened from under her. She then braced herself and walked slowly into the room. The shock on Jack's face was all Arianna needed to confirm that all this really did happen.

Right there before his very eyes his wife "The Lady Arianna Lawrence" beheld precious EXCALIBUR, the most famous of all swords.

MAGIC REALLY DOES EXIST
WHEN YOU TRULY BELIEVE
WITH YOUR HEART!

"THE END"

Or is it the beginning?

BIBLIOGRAPHY

An NBC HALLMARK television miniseries "MERLIN" starring award winning actor Sam Neill in the title role and Isabella Rossellini as The Lady Nimue.

Encyclopedia Britannica and Britannica on-line

Funk and Wagnall's on-line

"Knights" a book by Authors Julek Heller and Deirdre Headon.

Quote from the movie "The Wizard of OZ":
 "Toto, I don't think we're in Kansas anymore."

I have a heartfelt thank you to actor Sam Neill for igniting the fire and love in me for His Majesty King Arthur and the Prophet Merlin. They always had a special place in my heart.

My belief in these men and Excalibur has always held steadfast with me.

I thank my husband John and my children Andrea and John for supporting me in the telling of this story. May God bless all of them. I love them very much.

I also wish to thank my William Cullen Bryant High School Teachers-
George Chahallis and Lila Klauseman
Mr. Chahallis for instilling in me a love of history and Mrs. Klausemen for the love of the dramatic.

Most of all, I wish to thank God for helping me with all my struggles in life and for giving me the good Doctors and the staff at Queens Child Guidance and the Tourette's Foundation in helping my husband and my son.